OUR NEW NEOLITHIC AGE

Our New Neolithic Age

Trent Portigal

MANDELSTUCK EDITIONS

705, 10303 111 STREET

EDMONTON

For JEP.

1

The main street glimmers in predawn traffic. Snow fallen overnight has been reduced to a wet sheen on the asphalt, reflecting the white and red lights of passing cars and the green-yellow-red cycle of traffic lights. Streetlights' yellow glow barely makes an impression on car roofs and still-white sidewalks. As the sky lightens, Tony has the impression the streetlights are simply running out the clock until they can let go and shut down.

His grey Accord leaves the main flow of traffic, turning left during the brief moment offered by the changing traffic lights. The car immediately turns right down the alley behind the row of mostly dark shops and restaurants fronting the street and pulls into a gravel parking lot at the back of the second building in. Red brick walls and a stately white cornice give the postage stamp-sized structure a certain stature. The chain-link fence topped by barbed wire around the sides and rear add aloofness at the price of elegance.

Tony gets out of his car, hair and long coat blending with the greyness of the vehicle. He strolls back up the alley and around to the street, making his way to the front of the building. The fence does not leave enough room to pass directly to the front. Opening the padlocked gate is apparently an inconvenient option.

The front is far friendlier, with a couple trees, benches, bicycle rings and a sign before a façade with two narrow windows on either side of a bright red door half a dozen steps above the ground. No fence, not even an ankle-high ornate one, has been erected to dissuade visitors from traipsing through the flowers one might imagine in warmer seasons.

The sign, perched on two wooden posts between a tree and the bike loops, is like those with names and vacancies planted in the front lawns of all the four-storey walk-up apartments in the neighbourhood. In place of a fanciful, exotic name, the sign reads "Museum of." In lieu of tracks and panels indicating some combination of vacancies for one- to three-bedroom units, a slot for a four-sided block is built in.

Tony stands for a moment in front of the sign, absently gazing at it. The outward face of the block reads "Art." A passerby stops and looks at the sign over Tony's shoulder. Without paying attention to the person behind him, Tony releases a concealed clamp and pulls out the block. He turns it, revealing the words "Artifact," "Artifice" and "Artichoke" on the other three faces. He puts the block back with "Artichoke" facing out and re-engages the clamp.

"That just sounds awkward," the passerby opines. "'Artichoke Museum' would roll off the tongue far easier than 'Museum of Artichoke.'"

Tony shrugs without looking back.

"And what's the deal with 'Artichoke' anyway? Is it some sort of modern, post-Duchamp thing? Does putting an artichoke in an art museum make it art? But it's an artichoke museum now, so is whatever's in there suddenly an artichoke? Is that even possible? If you ask me, you should just leave it as 'Art.'"

"I don't believe you were asked," Tony replies in a voice rising just above the noise of cars passing on wet asphalt.

"Well, I should have been. And you should thank your lucky stars someone is willing to give you honest, constructive criticism. But then, do you really care? You're probably the inconsiderate clod who tramples the lovely blue flowers around the sign in the summertime just to confuse everyone with your inappropriate vegetables. You are probably behind the construction of this, this sign that makes light of the elegance of our native tongue."

Tony shrugs once more and turns his attention back to the sign. The passerby storms off just as the streetlights call it a morning. Commuting continues, indifferent to the art-artichoke debate. A minute later, Tony passes through the red door.

Light entering the single room through the two narrow windows is almost imperceptible. The pale glow from a large skylight makes more headway but still barely fills the space. The walls are hung with curtains. Each is fronted by a slender stand proffering a white cue card that adds a layer of words onto the opaque fabric. The floor is lightly painted concrete. A small table and stool by the door are the only furniture. A short stack of white brochures, ordinary letter-sized paper printed with an embellishment-free description of the exhibit, sit on one side of the table. On the other are a guest book and accompanying pen.

In the weak light, the floor and white paper seem dull, yet potentially brilliant. The curtains and everything else tend toward black, swallowing all the rays within reach. Tony's ambivalent greyness could be pulled in either direction. This would likely create a certain tension but for the foregone conclusion of the rising sun.

Looking closer, a small lamp in one corner also adds its modest weight to the light side of the balance. The curtains in its halo are clearly mauve, though not a mauve tending toward a similar tone as Tony in the twilight. An easy mistake to make, if one did not realize the curtains were theatrical and of French origin. Thus the cue cards.

Two teenage girls are sitting on the floor on either side of the lamp. One, Anna, is talking quickly and quietly. The other, Nadia, nods her head intermittently, either agreeing or slipping momentarily into the welcoming darkness of sleep. Neither pays attention to Tony's entrance. Tony, for his part, glances in their direction and sighs as he changes his shoes, leaving the flower stompers under the table.

He walks to the most obscure corner of the room, kitty-corner from the girls, passes between two curtains and down a staircase to the basement. A moment later, a strong light flicks on. It invades the main floor through the shifting gaps between the curtains disturbed by Tony's passage. The illumination reveals drapes of a variety of sombre colours, including black but not mauve. All the mauve curtains seem relegated to the one spot. Sounds of shifting boxes also make their way through the curtains, followed by Tony himself, coatless and with a cardboard box in his arms. He leaves the box in the middle of the floor.

Numerous trips to the basement later, a small mountain of boxes, each with a thick, black "artichoke" scrawled on it, has taken shape. At about the time the first layer was complete, the girls left. Anna had called back as they headed out the door: "Tony! I'll be back to help with the painting!" The words seemed to be only for form, without expectation of communication, let alone acknowledgement. They in any case did not influence Tony's methodical pace.

With the mountain built, Tony moves the brochures, guest book and pen to the stool and carries the table to the centre. He carefully unpacks one box, then another. The first several contain objects of artichoke-as-flower; a subsequent, larger number, artichoke-as-containing-a-heart; various artichoke-as-edible-vegetable follow. The final two boxes contain an Artie the Artichoke mascot costume and a dummy on which to put it. The collection might make an interesting case study in the art-artichoke debate.

As Tony assembles the dummy, his phone vibrates. He pulls it out of his pocket to see a meeting request entitled Museum Rationalization Review. He pauses, reflects, then starts tightening an elbow joint. The bolt resists, so he twists harder, puts more weight into turning it. He is so intent on forcing it that a minute goes by before he realizes it is misthreaded. He pulls back his arm to throw the wrench but stops himself. Instead, he walks several circles around the room. When he returns to the centre, he addresses the dummy: "Looks like you have some competition today."

The exhibition is clearly meant to take no more than a day to set up, even with an error or two thrown in. The small table seems much larger, displaying innumerable interpretations of the humble artichoke in such a way as to not appear crowded. The sunlight is noticeably fading by the time Tony returns a final time to the now-suited dummy, setting Artie in an enthusiastic mid-cheer. Despite the cue cards, the curtains take a second role, framing rather than being what attracts the visitors' gaze.

Tony stows the wrapping-filled boxes in the basement and takes his coat. He pulls on his flower stompers and exits the red door. An elderly passerby is taking a break on one of the benches. As far as Tony knows, it could be the same passerby as this morning. A bicycle is locked to one of the rings, the chain starting to rust in the wintry freeze-thaw. Definite signs of life, even if the museum did not see a single visitor all day. Tony goes around to the alley and melds with his grey car. As he turns the key, the first streetlights come to life.

2

"Tony! I'll be back to help with the painting!" Anna calls back as she closes the red door. She and Nadia descend the steps. A dishevelled man is sitting on one of the benches in the front yard. Beside him is parked a shopping cart filled with a miscellany of items, topped with a half-full green garbage bag. Anna approaches.

"Adam," she says. She pulls a six-pack of empty beer bottles out of her bag and hands it to him.

"Anna," he mumbles, taking the pack and putting it in the garbage bag.

Nadia ensures Anna is always between her and Adam as she makes her way to the sidewalk. She waits while Anna and Adam look at each other in silence.

"A fish-jesus is a very specific item," Adam finally says.

Anna nods, then joins Nadia on the sidewalk. The two walk up the street.

"You're weird," Nadia points out.

"You stayed awake almost the whole time."

"Weird can be entertaining, sometimes. I guess."

"It's not as if I want an actual fish-jesus."

"You've said."

"It's more of a general idea."

"A totem." Nadia mimics Anna's mannerisms.

"A totem."

"A symbol."

"A symbol."

"It's just that Adam wouldn't get it."

"Right, exactly. I don't really know what I'm looking for."

"Something weird and creepy, like Adam. You should just take a picture of him. Put it in your locker. Maybe draw a heart around it."

"Adam is very nice."

"In a weird and creepy sort of way."

"He's just homeless, down on his luck."

"Blah, blah. You say that every morning."

"It's true every morning."

"You should give him a full six-pack. See what happens."

"Like my brother would let me do that."

"But he's like a brain. Tell him it's for science."

"You can try."

"Me? Your brother is weirder than you are. Ech."

Nadia pulls out her phone and delves into the multitude of ongoing conversations she is having with people who are not there. Anna contemplates the puddles the melting snow leaves behind on the sidewalk, noticeable yet too shallow to be of any consequence. The storefronts they pass are a mix of boutique shops and restaurants, payday loan places, bars, and the occasional pawn shop. The buildings are bland, generic; a marginal working-class main street on the cusp of gentrification. The two girls turn off the street after three blocks, walk past a couple blocks of equally generic walk-up apartments and reach the set of boxes of various sizes stuck together that comprises their school. Despite being surrounded by other students, the girls' behaviour does not change until they are at their lockers. Nadia puts her jacket in her locker, slips her phone back in her pocket and joins Anna at hers.

"So, what's the heresy of the day?" Nadia asks.

Anna rips yesterday's page off her The Daily Calendar of Learned Heresies and reads today's blasphemy.

"The Adamites."

"That's too good. Let's all worship the weird and creepy."

"They worshiped like Adam before the fall."

"What does that even mean?"

"Naked."

"Really?"

"The early Christians had a nudist sect."

"I thought nothing really weird happened before the internet."

"It's not so weird."

"There you go again. Before the internet, you would've been stoned. Crucified if they found out about your fish-jesus fetish."

"Probably."

"English?"

"Counselor."

"Ech. Why can't they just let it go?"

"Covering their asses."

"Trig?"

"Yeah."

The bell rings. While students around them start heading to class, Nadia and Anna stay anchored in place.

"Okay," Nadia says, " now I'm the one screwed up in the head. I can't stop imagining Adam naked. I cannot describe how disgusting that is. Ech."

"So, you're saying you want to give Adam the beer bottles tomorrow."

"Stop it."

"Maybe attach a little note."

"Not funny."

"Written in pink, with little hearts for dots. A solemn and sacred confession, with a girly twist."

"I'm going to class." Nadia hurries off.

Anna reads yesterday's heresy, still in her hand:

Theodotists, Disciples of Theodore of Byzantium. He lacked the courage to be martyred, so renounced Christ. After, he preached that Jesus was only a man. He claimed to have only renounced the man and not the divine reality. Second century AD.

"Yeah," she says to herself under her breath, "courage is over-rated. Dying gruesomely; overrated, principles; overrated, heroism; definitely overrated..."

She saunters down the hallway, slowly making her way to the councillor's office and exploring the seemingly endless world of overrated concepts. Even when the councillor invites her into his office and she has settled into the chair, her train of thought keeps going.

"Anna Perenna, thank you for coming to see me this morning."

"It's a pleasure to be here," she responds distractedly.

"You are aware that sarcasm is a defence mechanism."

She bites her tongue, as she does every week. The only respons-es that ever come to mind are sarcastic.

"I am beginning to be concerned, to be completely open and honest with you. I still have not had a chance to sit down with your parents."

The councillor, Mr. Surget, has been concerned for seven weeks by Anna's count. Concern; overrated.

"I know they are busy," he continues. "I would be remiss howev-er to not flag the situation if it appeared you did not have adequate support at home."

Anna would usually say at this point that he had met with her older brother, effectively her guardian. Business, both pronuncia-tions; overrated.

"Your brother is not your legal guardian. To be frank, he is also perhaps not the best role model for you."

Here, she would point out that, as a doctoral candidate, Simon should be the ideal role model for the importance of education. Since her participation in the conversation is clearly unnecessary, she wonders if the overratedness of legal guardians should be left as a single expression or split into two. She decides to split it, just to be thorough.

"His commitment to education is commendable of course. None-theless, there are other qualities just as important." Surget pauses,

as if it finally dawns on him he has said all this before and the conversation has turned into a monologue. "All that said, how is your
ankle?"

The crux of the matter. As far as Anna is concerned, a good,
solid ankle cannot be overrated. Decent hand-eye coordination
would also be useful. It is not as if she and her friends had not done
worse things than climb onto the roof of the school. It was not the
first time they had climbed up there. It was the first time some of
them decided to hit gravel off the roof with a branch, the first time
she fouled a rock and managed to break a school window, the first
time she was panicked enough to not stick the landing coming back
down. A teacher overseeing some extracurricular activity or other
caught up with her as she was hobbling pathetically away. Effective,
or at least dignified, hobbling is not overrated.

"It's fine," she replies.

"I'm happy to hear that. And volunteering at the museum?"

"It's fine."

"What sort of things are you doing?"

"Painting the room for a new show."

"What is the exhibition going to be?"

"Dunno yet."

"When is it supposed to open?"

"Dunno."

"Museums usually have that sort of information available in advance, don't they?"

"Probably."

"Hum. I will bring that up next time I speak with Mr. Abbott."

"Oh."

"Trust must be earned. You know that. If I wasn't helping you
become more responsible and integrated in the community, I
wouldn't be doing my job. Climbing on the roof and breaking that
window shows very plainly you do not respect the institution. And
that was just the time you were caught. If your parents were here,
they would say the same thing: respect and responsibility. Right?"

Anna shrugs. Every second or third word that comes out of Surget's mouth is overrated. Maybe being thorough is too.

"Right?"

"Fine."

"Good. Moving on; no significant issues with your grades, your teachers do not have any particular problems. The consensus is that you are capable of more, if you decided to apply yourself."

Application; overrated. Anna waits for Surget to finish so she can leave. He always pauses here, giving her a chance to agree with him. She never does. She has more than enough application where it counts. What she needs is imagination; uncontrollable, scary imagination. She needs her own dog house; for the music to flow unbidden. Only, no need for it to be music, or a dog house, or fish-jesus. The details are unimportant. Scratch that: the details get in the way. Trees and forests and all that.

A stream of repetitive platitudes later, she finds herself in the blessedly empty and silent hallway. It is not a perfect, eerie silence; muffled voices do make their way through and under classroom doors. The noise is just enough to get a sense that the world of human interaction keeps humming along; that while she is in the middle of it, she is momentarily not a part of it. In the spirit of Theodore, she takes a Byzantine route through the intersecting boxes to her English class.

When she arrives, she listens to the hesitant voice of one of her classmates through the door.

Yet be most proud of that which I compile,
Whose influence is thine, and born of thee.
In others' works thou dost but mend the style,
And arts with thy sweet graces graced be;
But thou art all my art, and dost advance
As high as learning my rude ignorance.

Anna opens the door and enters as the teacher, Mrs. Sobeski, says, "Thank you, Gary. And thank you Anna for joining us. Auspicious timing Anna, as always. Your life will be all the poorer for having missed the inspired words of Shakespeare."

"Blame Mr. Surget," Anna responds, taking her place.

"We are out of time," Mrs. Sobeski addresses the class, then pauses while the bell rings. Chairs scrape as the students immediately get up to leave. "Tomorrow, we will discuss the structure of the English sonnet and you will all have a chance to write your own." As Anna passes, Mrs. Sobeski asks her to stay behind a moment.

"How is your ankle?"

Another cycle begins. Originally, Anna thought Sobeski cared about the ankle. It quickly dawned on her though that her teacher just wanted to set her guilt as the basis for what would come next. Since she herself had been playing a similar game, only with Surget as the target, it seemed fair. Still, she was not going to participate. She would just take whatever extra task Sobeski dished out. Getting to class five to ten minutes earlier would not change anything. She thought about testing it but could not bring herself to go to class earlier than she needed to.

"So, you want to skip the small talk? Okay. I was thinking about a page on the role of the muse in Shakespeare's sonnets. You can focus on number seventy-eight, if you happen to have caught the ending when you were coming in. For tomorrow."

Anna cannot decide if Sobeski is more self-aware than Surget or if she just does not take the same pleasure in hearing herself speak.

"Okay," Anna replies without enthusiasm.

Nadia is waiting in the hallway.

"You didn't need to wait," Anna says.

"Sure," Nadia replies, "but the shit Sobeski gives you is always worth a laugh."

"Shakespeare's muse, one page."

"Good thing it isn't your muse. Wouldn't want to admit to yourself how important Adam is to you."

"Adam's overrated."

"I guess for a homeless guy, he isn't too clever. Guess that's why he's still homeless. And why he can't find your totem."

"Sure."

"Not in the mood to talk. That's cool. Trig'll make it all better."

"Fuck off."

"Will do."

Geometry-Trigonometry, as taught by Mr. Chodkiewicz, is a mixture of slavish adherence to the textbook, a cult-like devotion to Pythagorean ideas and misogynistic social Darwinism. Art is rules, beauty is proportion, ugliness is as good as failure in the real world. Results on twice-weekly quizzes and overall performance are posted prominently as an ongoing competition. The top of the ranking is dominated by boys, the middle by girls and the bottom is roughly even. Chodkiewicz pretends the bottom does not exist. He spends five to ten minutes at the beginning of each class commenting at length on the top, with an occasional condescending nod toward the middle, before moving on to parroting the textbook, capped by some time to practice or a quiz.

"Shit," Anna says quietly to Nadia when they glance at the results for the last quiz. She managed to score above the comfortable, anonymous middle.

"The rules, my dear Anna, are your muse," Nadia whispers back as they take their seats. "You could be your own muse if it wasn't for your lazy eye and off-centre hunch."

"Ah, to be a symmetrical hunchback."

"Pray for another orb that doth not track."

"Doth not?"

"Kevin's reign in the top spot has come to an end," Chodkiewicz addresses the class. "Almost three weeks, not exactly a record. Not long enough to get past the probationary period for any job worth having. If I am not impressed, the partners would not be impressed, management would not be impressed."

He places himself in front of Kevin's desk and looks the boy in the eye: "You have set expectations, Kevin. You have shown your-self capable of being at the top. Three weeks may be inadequate but it's too long to be a fluke. Don't be a disappointment, Kevin."

"Speaking of flukes," he continues, making his way to the front of the class, "we have a blip by one of our perennial mediocrities, Anna Perenna. The School Board is worried you all, and particular-ly you girls, have issues with body-image. All I see day after day is that you are convinced you are some special flower, with a natural symmetry to call your own. I see that you spend hours watching clips on the web, learning the art of perfecting the illusion, hiding the bits where nature fell short. Board rules say I can't tell you how deluded the vast majority of you are. So I won't. I can tell you that the illusion wears through as time passes, no matter how much ef-fort you put in. Unlike the art I teach here.

"Charles," he spins and points, "you are back in the lead. But now you have competition. It's what makes life interesting; what will prepare you for the real world. You can't rest on your laurels. Now, to page hundred thirty-two." He walks back to his desk and opens his copy of the textbook.

"He didn't even look at you," Nadia points out as she and Anna leave the class. "And I found his whole deformed flower shtick un-inspired. The uselessness is ugliness rant is still his best work."

"He rarely looks at the deformed flowers."

"To be honest, we rarely look at him. Hard to daydream with his mug in the frame."

"You don't find him creepy?"

"Ech, yes! Adam is a suave gentleman in comparison. Adam the sleuth, tracking down a famed—even mystical—relic for the myste-rious, lopsided dame."

"Spoiler: the hunchback of Notre Dame is actually notre dame."

"Who tolls the bell, but is also the unfortunate soul for whom the bell tolls."

"Wouldn't that mean I'd be dead?"

"The mystery thickens." Nadia draws out the last word as she separates from Anna and pulls out her phone in one well-practiced move, heading to her theatre arts class. She is immediately replaced by Kevin.

"Chodkiewicz is an asshole," Kevin says.

"Yup," Anna replies.

"Don't let him get to you."

"Sure won't."

They lapse into silence until they reach the door of their social studies class.

"How's the ankle?" Kevin asks.

"My body hasn't rejected the transplant."

"Oh. That's good, I guess. I mean, the best we could hope for. Under the circumstances, I mean."

Anna does not bother responding. She chooses a seat surrounded by occupied desks to give herself some distance from Kevin. A fifty-minute episode in the long-running saga of the struggle among states and companies over resources and trade routes begins. The star of the day is the Hudson's Bay Company. Students are a passive audience, the teacher physically present but no more mentally engaged than the television through which the episode plays out.

She wonders, not for the first time, whether recounting these stories endlessly counts as repeating history. Her brother Simon thinks being doomed to repeat history in a classroom is a small price to pay to not be condemned to actually live in the midst of the misery and depravity of times past. He sees the fact they live in a time generally known as the Neolithic Era far more troubling. Any efforts to escape the loop are likely doomed from the start. Of course, she should hedge her bets and pay attention in class anyway.

Yet Shakespeare's muse compels her. No, Sobeski compels her. Shakespeare's muse fills her with jealousy. She does not want a muse that mends her style, that adds feathers to her wings. Her fish-jesus must be all her art. Though, somehow, in a way that still makes it hers. Just not the her stuck listening to a monotonous retelling of an imperialistic fur trade doubling as a British-French proxy war. It seems possible, if some unholy blend of Shakespeare and muse was able to write verse with their alien pen. So what if she is no Shakespeare and her fish-jesus is but a pale placeholder shamelessly borrowed from a young version of Kristin Hersh.

Fish-jesus was not even much of a muse for Hersh. It was not the source of the music that came to her unbidden. It was not the place where she gave in and allowed the music to overwhelm her. It was a common totem in a squat frequented by musicians and artists in the city. It was a symbol of the break between a relatively comfortable childhood and the strangeness and precarity permeating life as an artist just starting out. Despite Hersh writing about it, capturing it for posterity, it would never be a work to be studied, a rule to be followed or a story to be repeated as a cautionary or inspirational tale. It did not belong in this collection of boxes.

The Hudson's Bay Company story keeps coming back to a B-roll segment of fur traders canoeing along a river through a vast forest. The green of the vegetation is deep and rich, contrasting the pale wood of the canoes and the sun-speckled water. Anna ponders what colour fish-jesus was. She does not remember Hersh mentioning that detail. It could be forest green or aquamarine, just not the shade of obsessively managed and manicured lawns. A colour that would fit an object both deformed and divine. Not beautiful though; beauty is overrated.

Anna finishes the page on Shakespeare's muse as a quick epilogue of the Company's current corporate identity and challenges ties up loose ends. The essay is, as far as she is concerned, a masterful contemplation of artistic intent versus unconscious and external influences, as reflected in sonnet seventy-eight. It did not occur to her to read more than one sonnet or even search the subject on the web.

The art teacher generally leaves a room open at lunch so students can work on projects. She gives one of them the responsibility to make sure nothing untoward happens. These days, that has fallen to Martin, the budding artist of the term and Nadia's mostly on-again boyfriend. The room quickly became the preferred non-roof location for the group. Anna heads there when the bell rings, joined once more by Kevin.

"There was no transplant, was there?" Kevin asks.

"What can I tell you?"

"The truth."

"How long have you been thinking about it? Not all class?"

"No. I was canoeing on the Peace River last summer. Week-long trip with the family. Thought I recognized some of the shots. It was really fun, the trip."

"Do you do it a lot?"

"Camping, yes. Canoeing, not as much."

Nadia comes up behind them and interjects: "You're going to make Anna jealous. She almost never gets out of town. Can't even visit her parents in whatever exotic locales they find themselves. They say it's too dangerous."

"Wow, really?" Kevin asks.

"Turns out rare earth mines aren't all that close to family-friend-ly resorts. Whodathunkit?" Anna replies.

"This isn't like the transplant, is it?"

"The transplant?" Nadia inquires.

"It's not all rare earth, just rare. Anyway, everyone has known about the mining thing for a while," Anna replies. "It's not exactly new information. Apparently the brain transplant didn't take."

"Now you're just being mean," Kevin says.

"You'd be cranky too if your parents abandoned you for some unpronounceable metal halfway around the world," Nadia states. "Going skiing this weekend?"

"Yeah, just for a day in the mountains. You?"

"Probably. Cross-country, though. If there's enough snow."

The conversation between Nadia and Kevin meanders into the season's snow quantity and quality. After a quick stop at their lockers, the three reach the art room and coalesce with the other members of the group. Nadia takes the place Martin left free for her at the centre. Anna finds a more marginal position. The conversation expands and branches into a variety of topics, none of which capture her attention.

Some kids are actually in the room to work on projects. She aims for the middle ground between them and the group. Far enough from the group to not be a suck on the conversation but not so far as to be considered even more standoffish than normal. She opens the notebook she had out at the museum. A title, The Ear Stone Chronicles, sits at the top, blocky and underlined. Under it are thin, straggly ideas, adrift in the page's white sea.

3

In the short lull between the end of classes and the beginning of lacrosse and rugby practice, Martin and Nadia drag a metal garbage can to the edge of a covered school entrance. They climb from the can onto the overhang, from the overhang onto the roof of the single storey box. From there they take various ladders to the top of the third storey and choose a dry spot to sit where they cannot be seen from the school grounds or windows.

They face the building commonly known as the Monolith, a twelve-storey block in an orderly grid of four-storey walk-up apartments. The apartment roofs are painted white and black in a checkerboard pattern. The Monolith looks like the final piece on the board, crowned. Martin takes out his sketchbook and flips past dozens of drawings of that very view. Once he finds a fresh page, he draws it again. Nadia pulls a worn copy of The Errors of Young Tjaž out of her bag and starts to read.

After ten minutes, Martin breaks the silence. "You didn't really need to come up here, you know."

"I know."

"I mean, you don't care about the Monolith."

"I just want to spend time with you."

"We're not really together. You're in your book, I'm with my subject." He waves his pencil at the Monolith. "We're like my parents; mentally divorced from each other for as long as I can remember."

"Good thing we're just dumb kids then. Love may tear us apart, but hormones keep bringing us back together."

"Joy Division? Really?"

"You started it, with talk of passionless, disconnected old people.

Old people who gave the world baby Martin, no less. Ech."

"Let me finish this."

"I give you an hour, at most." Nadia pulls out her phone and sets the timer, glances at new messages and then puts it away. She re-opens her book.

"I can resist you."

"Sure," she replies without looking up from the page. She manages to read up to the moment when one of the narrators points out that the tale of Tjaž at his boarding school did not lend itself to an ending. The story had been absorbed by the school in a way impossible to erase. The account the book offers of young Tjaž suddenly seems thin to her, as if the portion above ground had been cut from the earth and then flattened and dried between the pages.

It takes twenty-six minutes for Martin to sigh, lower his sketch-book and shift closer to Nadia. She makes an effort to separate her brain from Tjaž and his boarding school, creating a void quick-ly filled with Martin's parents and other bits of daily miscellany. While her mental processes do their thing, her body leans into Mar-tin. They start kissing before Nadia pulls away.

"No," she declares, "can't do it."

"What? Why not?"

"It's like my mother's watching us." She gestures toward the Monolith. "She's all cold and detached; a corporate scientist observ-ing the thousandth test subjects in some study proving she really did build a better mousetrap."

"Never bothered you before."

"You never talked about your parents before."

"Yeah, shit. Now I'm not in the mood. And we're stuck up here until the jocks leave. And I can feel your mom's eyes on me. Your dad's too."

"He doesn't work there."

"What? I thought both your parents worked for United Mono-lith."

"One of the great ironies of life. Uni-lith has multiple locations.

He's at the distribution centre by the airport. The Monolith, as the kids call it, is pretty much only for R&D. It's not even the main R&D site though. Too many people live too close. What if something exploded?"

"Has anything exploded?"

"No idea. Probably. We probably live in a post-apocalyptic world and we don't even know it."

"I'm not sure an apocalypse is something that slips by unnoticed. If popular culture has taught me anything..." Martin reopens his sketchbook and starts drawing an exploding version of the Monolith.

"Maybe the explosion released just enough radiation to mutate us all, or a slow-acting disease, or some sort of genetically modified super-plant with blue flowers..."

"Then we'd be living the apocalypse." He looks up. "'The Creeping Apocalypse' would be a good band name." He refocuses on his drawing. "Once pretty much everyone is dead or transformed into horrible, deformed monsters, the post-apocalypse will be upon us. Where's the big R&D centre?"

"I think the name's been used before, maybe not for a band though. It's in the eastern industrial area."

"By the trailer park?"

"Yeah. And that massive church in the news a while back."

"The preacher with the private jet?"

"Yup."

"So, basically everything that would attract the anger of the gods in one place."

"Makes sense. Anna mentioned this neighbourhood used to be all houses and the Monolith a hospital. It all changed twenty or thirty years ago. Maybe there was an explosion or something, flattening everything."

"But that would've been before United Monolith moved in."

"They might have had something going on in the hospital."

"I don't buy it. Thought the apartments were older than that though."

"Slapped together before people started asking too many questions."

"And the school is definitely older."

"Lies!"

"Shush. Someone might hear you. Last thing we need is to get caught after the Anna incident."

"'The Anna incident'? Twisting her ankle is an 'incident' now?"

"You know what I mean. There were no issues coming up here to hang out, draw, smoke, whatever, until she got caught."

"You're acting like the teachers were a-okay with us coming up here before. We always had to sneak around."

"But not like this. Breaking that window..."

"It wasn't her idea."

"Kevin wouldn't have suggested hitting gravel if he wasn't trying to impress her."

"So every stupid idea he has is her fault because he has a crush on her? What the hell? And I don't recall you trying to stop him. You were egging him on and saying 'me next, me next' until it went south. Wow, and I thought parents were a turn-off."

Nadia gets up to leave. Martin grabs her arm.

"Practice isn't over yet," he says, "you have to wait."

"With you? No way." She pulls her arm free and takes the ladders back down to the small box. Carefully approaching the edge, she looks at the lacrosse players in the open space on the far side of the playing field still soggy from melted snow. The team is facing her direction; the coach away from her. She tosses her backpack onto a patch of yellow grass below, then hops off. When she touches the spongy ground, she collapses into a forward roll, snatches the backpack and pulls out her phone as she comes back up, transitioning effortlessly into a casual walk. A couple players applaud. By the time the coach turns around, there is nothing interesting to see.

Nadia weaves her way through the checkerboard of superficially identical apartment blocks, once more conversing with the absent. Every building has some differences: toys in yards; patio furniture and bicycles on balconies; drapes, curtains or flags in windows; repairs that don't quite match; incongruous, exotic names on the signs out front. A thousand minor details that escape notice by strangers passing through and give residents a sense of belonging and impermanence in equal measure. Residents who pay attention to their surroundings, at any rate.

Five blocks later, she approaches a spot where music is spilling out from between two buildings. She stops at the edge of one, waits for her phone to connect to the speaker, changes the music to St. Vincent and then turns the corner. The walls on either side are covered with climbing holds and graffiti blending verses of Saint Glinglin into an abstracted mural of a sinuous slot canyon. A couple people are bouldering. They do not comment on Nadia's arrival nor the imposition of her choice of music. She changes her shoes, slips on a pair of fingerless gloves and joins them in communal isolation.

She chooses the most aggressive routes, with holds regularly placed just beyond the reach of the tallest of the group that installed them. An occasional fall to the mat just pushes her to try harder, until her muscles stop following her commands. Even then, she takes an easy path, followed by a series of balconies and scrambles onto the roof of one of the buildings.

The roof, including the pipes and other protrusions but excluding the occasional puddle, is matte black. The vast plain of buildings drops off into a ravine on the south, groups of individual houses on the north and west. The eastern edge, across the main street, is marked by foothills of stubby apartment towers and thick grey office blocks, followed by downtown's lofty peaks. The Monolith, svelte yet strong, dominates the board more through example and aspiration than through brute force. The school resembles a pile of empty cardboard boxes left off to the side of a shop for reuse or recycling.

She looks toward the school; Martin is no longer where she left him. She sits heavily, then lays back. With some effort, she pulls out her phone but just sets it on her stomach without looking at it. She manages to stay still for five minutes before standing back up. Perhaps she would have lasted longer if she had young Tjaž to keep her company, instead of him being in her bag on the ground.

Once she has climbed down, one of her fellow boulderers breaks the silence: "The residents prefer we stay off the roofs. It isn't really safe to go that high without a harness."

"That's a waste. It's nice up there. Calm."

"True."

Nadia changes her shoes, takes off her gloves and heads home. The music cuts out when the connection between her phone and the speaker is lost. A moment later, it is replaced by the music playing when she arrived. That music fades away as she weaves through the checkerboard. She crosses a lawn littered with bright plastic toys, passes the obligatory sign announcing that The Dalmally has no vacancies at present and enters an apartment on the top floor.

"I'm home!" she calls out.

"Out here, Nads," her dad, Yi-Fu, calls back from the balcony.

"Ech! Don't call me 'Nads'! It's disgusting!" She drops her bag, kicks off her shoes, grabs her book and joins her father. He is on the narrow balcony in the middle of giving the barbecue a quick cleaning. "Yes, dinner! I'm starving. Please tell me we aren't going to wait for mom."

"Your mother texted. She is going to be late." He turns on the grill and they sit on the two foldable chairs beside the grill, set against the wall facing out. They idly observe the parking at the rear of the building, the alley and the parking of the facing, superficially identical, building.

"I don't know why she bothers. She's always late."

"Courtesy is why. She may have to spend more time at work than any of us would like but she hasn't forgotten about us. She doesn't take us for granted."

"Sure, whatever. That means we're not waiting, right?"

"Correct. Did you boulderlessly boulder after school? Commune with the great spirit of Saint Glinglin? Fondle Martin's nads?"

"Ech! So inappropriate!"

"Testicles?"

"You're not making things any better."

"I left some potatoes for you to peel in the kitchen."

"But all the nutrients are in the skin."

"And you're pooped, pooped right out."

"You're a child. The toys on the lawn are probably yours."

"I was too pooped to put them away. You still have enough energy for skiing, though?"

"Wouldn't miss it for the world. You're too out of shape to spend energy talking shit and I can check off the 'spend time with father' box. One less thing to feel guilty about when I put you in a home."

"So cruel. Want to bring out the meat?"

"Sure." Nadia brings out all the food destined for the grill, including unpeeled potatoes wrapped in foil. She sits back down, starts to pull out her phone, then changes her mind and picks up the book. Her dad goes in and out of the apartment; setting the table, putting a salad out and periodically checking the barbecue.

"I don't think my story will ever be substantial enough to seep into anything," Nadia says.

"What's that?" her dad asks as he passes by.

"What do you think happened to the memories in the walls of the hospital when it was torn down?"

"Don't follow," he calls from the kitchen. "What memories?"

"The patients' stories powerful enough to fuse with the building."

"Sounds kind of like Saint Glinglin, or the beginning of a ghost story."

"Do you think you'll leave a trace here, just by living your life?"

"Yeah, you. You?" He checks the grill, then stops to look at her.

"I mean, something in this place."

"Sounds like a subject to talk to your mother about." After another to and fro, he starts to take the food off the grill.

"She'll just dismiss it. I kind of hope my story just runs its course and then it's over."

"No statues then?"

"Statues are just a reminder after the fact; they aren't around early enough to absorb anything."

"I got nothing, except food. You're hungry, remember. And, seriously, talk to your mom."

They start eating at the kitchen table. Nadia pulls out her phone and puts it beside her plate. A third plate, covered, is left in front of one of the empty chairs. Fifteen minutes later, Nadia's mother Sara enters the apartment. In addition to her purse and a large bag, she is carrying a file box.

"Brought work home, did you?" Yi-Fu asks rhetorically. "Your plate should still be warm but let me know if it needs a reheat."

Nadia does not look up from her phone.

Sara shifts Nadia's bag and shoes to the side with her foot, then carefully puts the box and bag down. She takes off her shoes and arranges them neatly in line with the other footwear in the entryway closet. She then sits heavily down at the table, letting her purse drop to the floor beside her.

"Nadia," Sara starts, "you know that your phone isn't allowed... Oh, never mind. I don't care."

Nadia momentarily looks up. "Wow, that's generous of you."

"Hard day?" Yi-Fu asks.

"Not over yet." Sara takes off the cover and picks distractedly at her food. She brings an occasional forkful up to her mouth, chews and swallows without giving the impression she has tasted anything.

"Nadia has something to ask you."

"No, I don't," Nadia says, once more mostly absorbed by the absent.

"I heard rumours the big boss was in town today," Yi-Fu addresses Sara. "Did you see him?"

"Rumours? I told you he was going to be here. I told you my team had an important presentation."

"Oh, right. Sorry. At least I remember our anniversary." He forces a laugh. "How did it go?"

"I can barely follow that man's train of thought. The prototypes we were supposed to show him failed—but beforehand, luckily. Had they failed in front of him...I don't want to think about it. The whole day was scrambling to get something even mildly impressive together for him. Add to that trying to translate opaque Beauty and the Beast—nineteen-forties version, of course—references into something a normal human being can understand."

Sara's voice picks up speed through her short rant, before falling to a low monotone.

"So, tonight, I need to do what I was supposed to have done today. Thanks for dinner. How was your day?"

"You're welcome; it was a team effort. Nadia was a great help. Just this once, I think you need to get some work done at the table."

"Just this once?"

"The exception. What's the point of the rule otherwise?"

"Okay. Just this once"

The rest of the meal passes in silence. Sara reviews proposals, Nadia keeps abreast of the minutiae of the lives of her peers and Yi-Fu savours the food he made.

4

Driss Rehg, CEO of United Monolith, stands with hands clasped behind his back, gazing out the window of a small corner meeting room at the top of the Monolith. The checkerboard below gradually comes into focus as the morning sky brightens. Sara sits at the round table in the room's centre. A closed laptop and two phones, three perfectly aligned rectangles, are arranged on the table opposite her. Nothing declares explicitly that the room is serving as Rehg's temporary office, yet it is somehow obvious. When the streetlights blink out, as if on cue, he starts talking.

"I don't get back here enough," he sighs. "The neighbourhood isn't perfect. The high school ruins the geometry of the board. The apartments have not aged as well as they might have. Did you know there used to be a hospital where the Monolith is now?"

"Yes."

"So many bad memories for a place of healing. A lot of mistreatment; perhaps even an aura of death, if that isn't being too melodramatic."

"There were a lot of issues."

"I remember hearing an interview on the radio once. The guest was being asked about her reaction to Beauty and The Beast, 1946 version. I don't recall who the guest was, just that she saw it during its original release and that it stuck with her decades later. She loved the movie. At the same time, she was disappointed when the Beast turned back into a prince at the end. She was not the only one in the theatre with that sentiment. The audience apparently had an audible reaction to the transformation and three or four others clearly aired their disenchantment. They were the minority but she was not alone."

He pauses for a moment before continuing.

"The banter between the two leads regularly played off his brutish form. Belle's take on his appearance did not evolve from it being an impediment against seeing his real self to it being superfluous. She caressed him as one would an animal companion to show her affection. When he made an observation about it, she pointed out that he was a beast. His form was central to their relationship.

"This building is not the monolith from 2001. It is not a miraculous oddity, nor a square-jawed prince surrounded by adoring rabble. It is still the beast. Only now it controls its base instincts rather than being a slave to them. It still hunts and kills, but with honour. The community reaps the benefits. So many practices of the hospital were shameful; the goal of fighting disease and improving people's lives was not. And we are not so different. It is all too easy to slip into old habits when reaching for noble goals. It is all too easy to ignore the atrocities in the cobalt and neodymium mines. Our Neolithic Age is haunted by the very ore on which it is built.

"I had the neighbourhood transformed when the Monolith was built. The apartments have not aged as well as they might have. And sure, it was practical; we needed good-quality staff housing nearby. It was also the proof of concept for our property management subsidiary. But it provided everyone with clean, modern and affordable homes. Well, mostly everyone. It's still market housing, after all."

Driss pauses again.

"Where was I? Oh yes, the modern Beast is a sort of apex predator who dominates other predators. The movies don't show him chasing after deer or rabbits—prey that just happens to be cute and apparently inoffensive. 'Apparently' being the operative word. The damage those creatures do would turn your head. The 1946 version made the chase somewhat family-friendly, the Beast's ears perked up when he heard prey nearby; he was noticeably distracted, his nature pulling him away from Belle. He was like a pet dog pulling on its leash to chase a squirrel. Carcasses were shown, mind you, but not the kill. It was clear without being explicit. He was just not the same person at the end, without that grounded, basic struggle.

"United Monolith is the apex predator. The board is cleared of our competition." He waves toward the checkerboard buildings, stopping at the school. "We should have done something with the school.

"We are about to acquire Consolidated Aerolithics. It is time to bring you into the loop."

"It's hard to believe the Perennas would give up control," Sara says, surprised.

"That changed six months ago, more or less. We've been negotiating ever since, slowly and patiently."

"Are they going to stay on?"

"This is still confidential. I understand your Nadia is friends with their daughter. Not even a hint about this can come out."

"Of course."

"Yes, they plan to stay on. They did not start the company to spend their time managing terrestrial mines. If they did, they wouldn't have named it Consolidated Aerolithics. No, they wanted to focus on mining technology suitable for the moon, asteroids and the like. They were just ahead of their time. They might still be but we are betting the time is right around the corner. Rapid advances in commercial rocketry in the past decade have changed the game. The focus for the time being is on putting satellites into orbit and delivering payloads to the IIS, yet every company in the game has grander ambitions.

"Consolidated Aerolithics is going to become a division of United Monolith. All the terrestrial assets will be moved over to Monolith. Everything that will allow us to be the first to start commercial mining operations off-planet will go to Aerolithics. A win-win, if there ever was one."

"So, why am I being brought into the loop now?"

"You are our most senior manager permanently at this location. We need someone on the ground to chase after the squirrels. The metaphor is approximate, I grant you, but I like it. United Monolith may have local operations, we may have provided more affordable market housing than any other group, we may have made a substantive, positive difference, but we are also a Beast too far removed from human-scale to be loved. Normally, that's a good thing. It's the only way to be taken seriously by the Beasts in other sectors.

"The Perennas have gone the other route. They lead a multinational concern and are almost entirely absent from local attention, yet Consolidated Aerolithics has still managed to be loved as a local business that has exceeded all expectations. We are aspirational but can't compete against reaching for that shooting star. Looking closely, people might be turned off, even disgusted, by the idea of exploiting the moon commercially, let alone the realities of the African mines they run. No one is interested in looking closely.

"They come off as the cute herbivore the modern Beast can't touch without giving offense."

"I'm sure marketing can put something together to expose their less-than-innocent side."

"I'm sure they can too. That doesn't work for me. No, what I want is some symbolic local investment."

"Okay. We have a great science and technology outreach program we can build on."

"Yes, you should do that. Also, you need to get an agreement together to take over control of a museum. A management agreement should do, though buying or leasing it is not out of the question. The two ideas can go together."

"Do you have a particular museum in mind?"

"The one on 124th Street."

"I'm not familiar with it. Is it a science museum?"

"I don't know. Probably not. I think the next exhibit is supposed to be hinges."

"Hinges?"

"Maybe there's something scientific about them. Or technological."

"I guess, maybe."

"It doesn't matter. It's been preempted. Did you know United Monolith's first symbol was a shield?"

"No."

"A massive, shining shield. It doesn't make any sense. A spear perhaps; something aggressive. But the leadership at the time went for defense. To throw people off, perhaps. Yes, that must be it: a feint.

"I asked logistics if we had anything lying around in a warehouse somewhere that was expensive and seemed meaningful. It turns out we have a giant golden—as in solid gold—shield. It's going to be delivered to the museum. You should confirm when."

"But we don't have an agreement in place."

"We do actually, but only covering security. Wouldn't want to leave a mass of gold somewhere without taking some precautions. It's a show of good faith, that we're serious about investing in the institution, in the city and the region in a way that goes beyond our core interests. A solid basis for you to do your thing."

"Speaking of my thing, is the expectation that I split my time between research and this?"

"Your priority is still research. The deadlines haven't changed. I am looking forward to the demonstration this afternoon."

"Yes, of course. I will have a project outline drawn up regarding the museum for your review. I am assuming law has been informed I am now in the loop and can give me a copy of the security agreement. Is there anyone else I should be talking to at this stage?"

"I will send a message to law and forward you the name of someone in the Mayor's Office."

"Thank you. If that's all, I will see you this afternoon."

"Yes, that will do for now."

Sara shuts her computer, rises from her chair and turns to leave. She turns back to add:

"I hadn't realized how complex Beauty and the Beast was or that you knew so much about it. That was very interesting."

"We may live in the Neolithic Era, Sara, but that does not mean we should live like cavemen."

"That makes sense."

Sara takes the stairs down two flights and heads north to her office on the dark side of the Monolith. The increasingly dominant fluorescent lights, doubled with surfaces painted with light, unobtrusive colours, give her an unhealthy pallor. Two of her lead scientists, Hassan and Gail, are waiting for her when she arrives in her personal box, surrounded by neat stacks of thick reports and studies.

"This can't be good," she says as she sits behind a small, empty desk and plugs in her computer.

"About the demonstration this afternoon," Hassan says nervously. "We can't do it. It just won't work. The magnets all lost their coercivity..."

"They are magnets no more," Gail interjects.

"They weren't performing all that well this past week," Hassan continues, "but all the signs pointed to operability limitations at high temperatures. We were expecting that, a predictable side-effect of not using terbium in the compound..."

"Or dysprosium," Gail interjects. "And I predicted the demagnetization."

"Or dysprosium of course. But we could keep the rotor speed down, add coolant—it would just be a proof of concept that could be ramped up once the molecules are further reduced and more of the neodymium is pushed to the outside."

"You are telling me now we don't have a functioning motor?" Sara asks, somehow becoming paler.

"Kind of difficult to have a permanent magnet motor without permanent magnets," Gail says. "I've been telling everyone for weeks. Even had a wager on it. So I won, if that's any consolation."

"But it's theoretically possible," Hassan points out. "We're almost there. Just not today. You have to put it off."

"Driss Rehg is already here," Sara sighs. "And he is leaving for China tomorrow. Even if the motor worked, it would be hard to put it into production without the mining rights for the raw materials.

What are our other options?"

"I can show him how it is supposed to work," Hassan offers.

"Not a good option."

"Most research projects have been moved to other centres. This is the only one still here this far along."

"Gail, what was the wager?"

"A hundred. Oh, you mean what I was betting on? That we couldn't go past a thirty percent drop in neodymium this year for PM motors. Turns out twenty-eight percent was the limit. Could have probably cut it a bit closer, won a lot more money, but that would've been tempting fate."

"We're doomed," Hassan says. "The project is going to get cancelled. If I'm lucky, I'll be added as a junior to another team, one that gets results."

"You have to come up with something," Gail adds. "I bet beer money—not enough for my retirement."

"I'm thinking," Sara replies. "Okay but we do have working motors."

"Not here," Hassan states.

"No but at the facility at the edge of town. They are prototyping reduced neodymium motors. I'm sure of it."

"Sure," Gail says, "but twenty, maybe twenty-two, percent reduction. Not all that impressive."

"Rehg hasn't seen them, right?"

"No. They started testing six months ago. He hasn't been in this neck of the woods in, what? nine months? A year?"

"And they are based on work done here? I know they are. I mean, can one of you speak to the details?"

"I have the slides," Hassan says. "Yes, I can add them, give a broader overview, point to where we are going. We still aim to go beyond thirty percent this year."

"Don't!" Gail cries. "Just don't tempt fate like that. It's not healthy. You're going to give yourself another anxiety attack."

"Maybe avoid that sort of detail for now," Sara says. "We'll meet after and go over how the timelines need to be modified."

"Oh!" Hassan says. "I forgot. We can't move the prototypes. We'll never get them here."

"We go there," Sara clarifies. "It honestly never crossed my mind to try to bring them here."

"Right, of course. That's good."

"Okay, I'll call ahead and give them the news. Gail, can you drive there now and help them set up? Hassan, work on the presentation. Then we'll pack up everything we might need, head over and do what we can to make it all look less last-minute. I'll come back for Rehg when the time comes. It's a good thing the prototype team is easy to get along with."

"What does it matter?" Gail asks. "They work for you."

"Can you drive over there?"

"Yeah, not a problem."

"Thank you. You do realize things go smoother if your team is on board with what needs to be done. Pulling rank only goes so far."

Gail shrugs. "My underlings will share in my winnings. I should write a management book entitled Beer equals Loyalty. With an equal sign."

"Things might also go smoother if you didn't bet against the success of projects your team is working on."

"Totally on board with you there, so long as success is possible. Bit of a quibble, but nothing kills morale like impossible goals, shooting for the proverbial stars. If that's the case, might as well get some beer out of it."

"Can I go?" Hassan asks. "The presentation..."

"Right, yes," Sara responds.

"And I'll be off too," Gail says.

"Thank you. Let me know if there are any more complications as soon as possible."

Once the two scientists are gone, Sara walks slowly around her office. She stops at a pile of proposals with a pale yellow sticky note on top. The note reminds her the bids are supposed to be reviewed by the end of the day. She breathes deeply, returns to her desk and dials the facility at the edge of town.

5

The apartment building where Anna and Simon ostensibly live with their parents only contains two four-storey units, side by side. The Perenna side is a hive of activity. Simon is busy in the kitchen packing a large cooler. Fellow grad students and others more or less linked to the academic world stack folding lawn furniture, boxes of alcohol and food, and a wide variety of miscellaneous items, such as toilet paper, blankets, pillows and slippers. Helen, a fellow student and Simon's girlfriend, counts what they have amassed.

"I think this might be too much," she says quietly, then repeats herself so everyone can hear.

"No such thing," Max replies, adding another box to the pile.

"No such thing!" Simon yells from the kitchen.

"I just can't believe we're doing this again," Pris says with enthusiasm, pulling a chair off the pile, unfolding and sitting on it. "Tony didn't seem so into it last time."

"I find it hard to believe it is a 'thing' to begin with," Helen states.

"Oh, right, you haven't been around long enough to experience Artichoke Day," Max reflects. "It's actually not that big a deal, more of an excuse for a soirée."

"Simon and Tony can take it pretty seriously," Pris adds, "but that just adds to the entertainment for the rest of us. Unless they get too religious-y. Then they can be a drag."

"It seems like that's the reason it died," Max continues. "Tony thought we were having too much fun is what I understand. We were supposed to take the artichoke more seriously, I guess."

Simon and Saul enter, carrying the cooler between them.

"This is a lot of stuff," Simon admits.

"See?" Helen says.

"I'll text Tony, have him swing by. We can load up his car."

"Or we could take less..."

"No, no. It's about the right amount; adequately excessive."

"Which is why I'm surprised it's happening," Pris steers the conversation back. "Not that I'm not happy about it. Sometimes I need an extra push to get out of the house."

"Simon, what's the story?" Max asks.

"Museum restructuring," Saul says, Simon being too busy arranging things with Tony and other guests to respond.

"What?!" Pris and Max ask in unison.

"Yeah, the place might be shutting down. Honestly, it's a surprise it's lasted this long."

"Which explains the excess?" Helen asks.

The others shake their heads.

"Five minutes," Simon announces. "We'll pack the car, then you should all head over. I have to wait for my sister."

"I'll stay too," Helen says.

"Take stuff to the curb?" Pris asks, already picking up a box. The others follow her lead. "We still need an explanation for the 'museum restructuring.'"

"But it can wait until later," Max adds.

The mountain is slowly shifted onto the spotlessly and unseasonably green front lawn. A couple minutes later, Tony's grey Accord pulls up. He pops the trunk and gets out to help pack. His grey clothing has been replaced by a matte black ensemble, creating the illusion that his skin and hair are lighter, that they reflect more of the streetlights' yellow glow than they did that morning.

A passerby stops next to Tony and says, "I'm sorry for your loss."

"Thank you," Tony replies, a box full of clinking bottles in his hands. "It has been a trying time."

"You know, alcohol isn't the best solace for sorrow."

"Excessive solicitude isn't exactly a super solace for sadness either, I daresay." Tony puts the box in the trunk.

"You are obviously grieving, so I will turn the other cheek." The passerby walks off, visibly annoyed.

The Accord is quickly packed. Simon and Helen sit on the stoop as it pulls away. They watch Pris and the rest of the group walk up the street, the car only having enough room for Tony and boxes. Helen shivers, goes inside for another layer, then rejoins Simon.

"Should have kept a blanket," she says.

Simon nods lazily.

"Seems like Artichoke Day has a whole mythology behind it."

"I guess. When Tony took over the museum, he didn't like having to close between exhibits. So, he put something together people could still come and see, and he could easily work around. He probably found an artichoke collection on some classified site or at a garage sale, and built things up from there. Not much more to it. It was always a bit silly, which is just the thing for a bunch of shut-in wanna-be academics to let off steam. What did you do before you transferred here?"

"Nothing so elaborate. Is the museum going to close?"

"Tony thinks so but I'm not sure a decision has been made."

"It would be too bad if they did close it."

"I suppose. Probably makes sense though, practically speaking. Can't be cheap to maintain and they don't seem to get many visitors. Not that I'm the best person to talk about practicality. Ah, Anna!"

Anna walks up, taking the path rather than cutting across the unreasonably green grass. She greets Helen and her brother without enthusiasm.

"Buck up," Simon says, "It's Artichoke Day!"

"What?!" Anna asks perking up. "Tony was starting to put them out when I left, but he didn't say anything. I didn't think it was a thing anymore."

"Go inside, freshen up, whatever else you need to do. We'll be waiting out here."

"Not if it gets any colder," Helen says.

"Whatever. We'll be waiting for you somewhere."

Anna makes a quick turnaround and the three start walking toward the museum.

"Your Mr. Surget called again," Simon tells his sister.

"Of course he did."

"I don't know what he wants from me. I've told him a hundred times you're fine, walking the straight and narrow, contributing to the community, et cetera, et cetera. None of it makes a dint. Every week it's the same story and it's getting really old."

"You're not mom and dad."

"So?"

"So he won't back off until he talks to them. And they're never around. Can't even get them on the phone anymore. I kind of get it, even if Surget thinks he's God's gift to the poor, troubled youth of the world. Every time I meet with him I want to, I don't know, throw something at him. No, not really. I just ignore him. Let him run on, hear himself talk. It's not worth it."

"You get it?"

"We have deadbeat parents. It's great for a while; can't beat the freedom, the company keeps paying for everything, everyone who knows is jealous. But then, I can't tell you how many times I've wondered why our parents never want to see us. How many times have we talked about it?"

"A lot."

"Right? Surget's right though. Who cares what the reasons are. They're our parents. They have responsibilities. If Surget's an asshole, what does that make them? I can't even find the words."

"I know what you mean."

"Horrible or selfish or... But then I feel stupid. Wouldn't deadbeat parents leave us with nothing? What if they're doing amazing things to clean up the mines in central Africa? I've heard the horror stories. How horrible and selfish would I have to be to bitch about them not being here to clean up after my idiotic, childish mess."

"They are still your parents," Helen says. "You're neither stupid nor selfish."

"Helen's right," Simon adds. "I feel that way and I'm an adult."

"Technically an adult," Anna points out.

"It's the questionable maturity," Helen confirms. She addresses Anna, "Had he twisted his ankle, he would have just sat there whining."

"He told you about the ankle?"

"Oh, I'm sorry..."

"No, it's fine. Embarrassing perhaps but it's time to move on, laugh about it even."

"Whatever," Simon says. "Sulk for as long as you need to. And I'm here for you, even if we have established thoroughly I am not, you know, enough."

"I think if we've established anything, it's that being here counts for a lot," Helen suggests.

"Yeah," Anna agrees. "You're mainly not enough for Surget and that shouldn't be your problem. Besides, you've got to be the reason he hasn't called child and family services yet, despite his threats."

The three arrive at the Museum of Artichoke. A couple acquaintances of Simon and Helen are sitting on the benches out front, smoking and talking quietly. The narrow windows in the façade emanate a warm light. They paint lines of pale yellow across the oversaturated lawn and emphasise the relative darkness in which everything else is wrapped. Only the clean white line of the cornice and the dull red of the door resist. After a series of quick greetings, the three head to the door. A curtain brochure with "Private Function" written in block letters on the back is taped to it.

An eclectic collection of lamps lights the room just brightly enough to tease out the colours of the curtains still hung around the edges. The thin stands have been repurposed as a largely symbolic barrier around the artichoke exhibit, leaving a certain ambiguity as to which side is hidden behind the fabric—the walls or the festivities. Food and drink tables are set up kitty-corner from each other. Another brochure with "toilet" written in the same block letters and an arrow pointing down is taped to a curtain at the corner with the stairway leading to the basement.

Chairs, blankets and pillows are scattered throughout the space, generally oriented toward the artichoke table. Small groups of people are scattered and oriented in the same way. Max and Pris are stationed at the entry behind a pile of shoes covered in varying amounts of mud and another of clean slippers. They ensure random people do not crash the party and shoes are exchanged for slippers before invitees go any further. They also seem to be in charge of the atmospheric music flowing from a series of connected speakers around the room.

Tony is sitting on a chair in the mauve corner with Saul and several others, his back toward the curtains. Unlike the black curtains, the warmth of the light does not soften the starkness of his clothes. Simon looks over at him as the three change their footwear. Slippered, Anna makes a beeline for the food table. The other two linger at the entrance.

"Now I understand the slippers," Helen says to no one in particular. "You don't want to get mud everywhere and the concrete is too cold for stocking feet. And the lamps too. You guys did a great job setting up!"

"How's Tony doing?" Simon asks Pris and Max.

"Thanks, Helen! I can never tell," Pris says.

"Yeah, we don't have much of a baseline to go on," Max adds.

"Did anyone find the communal pig?" Simon wonders.

"How many people are here?" Helen asks. "Sorry, a pig now?"

"Nope," Max replies to Simon.

"Forty maybe, and yup," Pris responds to Helen. "Small room; it fills up quickly."

"But the pig?" Helen insists as she and Simon make their way to the drinks table.

"Goes with the whole Saint Anthony motif, Tony's alter ego. He's the only full-timer at the museum, basically a hermit. So we got him a plush pig as a sort of museum-warming present. In various stories, Saint Anthony had a loyal companion pig as he faced his temptations. Only, it was actually a communal pig. So it got put in a box with a bunch of other stuff, was brought out with the slippers and the lamps on Artichoke Days and other occasions. Then we lost it. I was hoping we'd find it again, what with the museum probably closing down. For old time's sake."

"A twisted sort of logic."

"Case in point for why I'm an unfit guardian."

Helen looks around for Anna. She sees her by herself on a blanket close to the artichoke flowers, leaning back against a pile of pillows, a notebook on her lap and a crumb-filled plate beside her.

"Maybe we should go talk to Anna. She seems lost in her own world," Helen suggests once they have a drink in their hands.

"I'd like to talk to Tony first."

"Okay, join us after."

Simon grabs a chair and takes a seat beside Tony in the mauve corner.

"Don't choke, Artie!" an acquaintance Simon is fairly sure is named Tim says.

"You want that to be a thing?" Saul asks, incredulous.

"It makes sense. He's a mascot with 'choke' in his name. Athletes are notoriously superstitious. There has to be some ritual that makes him lucky somehow."

"I think it's hopeless," Alex, a junior lecturer, argues. "He's doomed to choke. It's his nature."

"A frog-scorpion scenario?" Saul asks.

"No way," Tim says. "It's just an English gloss. A random word someone gave the object. Nothing to do with its nature."

"Sure," Alex responds, "if it was a real artichoke or some other more or less natural occurrence. But it's a character created by someone—an English speaker in an Anglophone context—with the poetry of the name—in English—part and parcel from the get-go."

Simon leans over to Tony as the debate continues: "Museum Rationalization Review?"

"Simon, how are you?"

"Can't complain."

"So many new faces."

"Yeah. The PhD students and faculty stick around for a while. Every time you blink, there's a new crop of Master's students and postdocs."

"Shouldn't you have finished up by now?"

"Probably, but the market sucks these days. There's no hurry. Talk to me about the review."

"You already know the story."

"I know it's not the first time. I know the building is a former substation that had been sitting around empty for decades, that the museum was created when council gave the nod for the neighbourhood to be razed. It was a sop for the heritage groups, so some of the elements of the neighbourhood could be saved and put on display. It's never made much sense; the elements don't mean much pulled apart and stuck on a wall. On the other hand, it was promised and no one has been willing to make the unpopular decision to shut it down. But you think this time is different. Why?"

"Enough time has passed. The building is going to have to be condemned if they don't throw a lot of money at it to fix it up. The main museum and archives has just been modernized; closing this place was one of the justifications for the investment. Nobody really cares anymore."

"We care."

"You care about the artichokes. Do you even know what the next exhibit is?"

"Can't say I do."

"Hinges. Interesting, right?"

"Well..."

"They're mass produced, from a catalogue. Not like the unique ones you still find sometimes in farm buildings. Not exactly what made the neighbourhood special."

"Maybe if they were shown in a unique way..."

"That would end up being an art installation, which is fine as far as that goes. Not exactly reflective of their use in the neighbourhood."

"That's it then. One last Artichoke Day."

"For old time's sake. Give the old hermit some temptation before he's transferred to central."

"You do realize it doesn't work if you invite the vices into your house. They need to wear you down, force their way in."

"The house crumbling isn't enough? Allowing you in isn't a sign of my faltering faith in the institution?"

"You make fair points."

As if to test the points, a large, weathered man in a well-tailored midnight-blue suit comes through the red door. He looks around, disoriented. Max and Pris engage him in conversation.

"Ooh," Simon says, looking at the newcomer. "Vice or virtue?"

"Anyone here tonight has got to be vice," Tony replies. "But he looks like he's on another level, a well-heeled heretic or even the devil himself."

"Too bad we don't have the communal pig to sniff him out."

"Right, the pig. Another reason my faith is floundering, no doubt."

Pris points toward them and the man starts walking through the labyrinth of chairs and pillows to the mauve corner. Curiosity gnaws at both Pris and Max, inciting them to follow behind and stay in earshot.

"Seems serious," Simon opines.

"He can't tempt me if he doesn't know where I am."

"I always thought all us skeptics and corrupters had a built-in compass. We might have read him wrong. He looks like he's all business, which could be a sign of insufferable virtue."

The man stands in front of the group, continuing to scan the room. "Is one of you Tony Abbott?"

"Me," Tony says. "What can I do for you?"

"My name is Tarik Williams. I'm with United Monolith, security. I have a delivery."

"Sure, I can sign for it."

"It's a large crate, sir. It can't fit through the front door. I need the keys for the back gate, the service door opened and a space on the floor, say two by three metres, cleared."

The conversations die down and the music is lowered. Everyone in the room pays attention to the exchange.

"I haven't heard anything about this," Tony says, pulling out his phone and looking for messages and emails he might have missed. "Give me a moment."

"What's in the crate?" Simon asks.

Tarik does not respond.

"Nope," Tony concludes, "I don't have anything."

"Perhaps you need to call someone."

"At this time? Clearly, you're not familiar with the bureaucracy."

Tarik looks at him, making it clear without a single word that the security officer has an assignment and that he is not going to be turned away with a flippant remark.

"Okay, alright. I'll call someone." Tony calls several people in the hierarchy before someone picks up. That someone has vaguely heard of a meeting between the Mayor's Office and United Monolith touching on heritage. Nothing formal had been communicated though, so she has to confirm.

"Why is a security guy doing a delivery?" Tony asks Tarik while they wait. "Is it valuable?"

"Do you want something to eat while you wait?" Max asks, trying to soften Tarik's demeanor and lighten the mood.

"You can take some out to your crew," Pris ventures.

"Thank you. We're fine," Tarik responds after a pause.

As the minutes tick on with no sign the festivities will resume any time soon, people start to trickle out. Max and Pris migrate back to the entry to thank them for coming and help with the slipper-shoe transition.

"There's going to be lots of leftovers," Max sighs, coming back to the mauve corner after the exodus.

Half an hour goes by. Tarik checks his watch.

"I warned you," Tony says. "Bureaucracies don't work quickly. I'm surprised I got anyone on the phone. And why aren't you talking to your people to help sort this out?"

"My orders are clear."

"Well that's helpful."

Tarik scans the room once more. Pris is folding chairs and putting blankets and pillows away to encourage those left to congregate in one area. The blanket Anna and Helen occupy becomes a peninsula of artichoke island. Pris adds extra pillows to it as a break against the cold concrete sea.

"Okay," Tarik decides. "We are going to drop off the crate. If a mistake has been made, it can be picked up later."

"No, that doesn't really..." Tony begins, but Tarik is already striding to the back to open the door.

"They still don't have the key for the gate," Simon points out.

"Do you think that'll stop them?" Saul asks.

Everyone in the group shakes their head.

Tarik opens the door, letting in a gust of cold air.

"If that isn't foreshadowing..." Simon says, shivering. "At least we're warm, friendly vices."

Men; some in lined overalls, others in overcoats; are milling around the back of what appears to be a five-ton truck, save for a couple extra sets of wheels. Tarik directs them to cut the chain securing the gate and back the truck to the building. Bolt cutters appear almost instantaneously. The truck is in place moments later. One of the men in overalls lowers the tail loading platform to the height of the museum floor. Another opens the vehicle, revealing a forklift and a single crate that barely fits the width and height of the box.

"Shouldn't we be moving the artichokes?" Saul asks.

Tarik calls back, "The, whatever that is, needs to be moved."

"It can't just be taken down in an instant," Tony protests.

The group stands frozen, then breaks into a frenzy of activity.

As the United Monolith crew measures the space and lays a track to the centre of the room, half the group descends to the basement to get the boxes Tony unpacked earlier in the day. The other half starts shifting the exhibit toward the front of the room. Simon helps Anna and Helen dismantle their peninsula.

One of the crew starts up the forklift, filling the room with the odour of propane. With the guidance of several others, he carefully pulls the crate out of the box without scraping the sides. As he goes over the loading platform, it lightly grazes the top of the box.

The group, slightly panicked, is far more clumsy. Pieces are haphazardly wrapped and stuffed into boxes. Artie is ripped in several places as he is taken off the dummy. Pithy remarks have given way to silent application. In the midst of the activity, an artichoke-as-flower falls off the table and rolls toward the back of the room. Anna notices at the last instant and calls out. The crewmembers guiding the forklift look toward her in incomprehension. She points; one of the men realizes what has happened and signals the driver to stop. The driver reacts quickly but it is already too late. He moves the vehicle forward, revealing an unrecognizable mess of fabric, plastic and ceramics.

Both the crew and the group pause, not knowing how to react. Tarik breaks the silence with orders to the crew. "Clean it up." He points to a man in an overcoat. "Stand here, make sure nothing else rolls back." He then joins the group in order to speed up the packing. The crew gets back to work. The group looks at him as if expecting, if not a promise of compensation, at least an apology. When it does not come, they turn to Tony. He continues wrapping and boxing without a word, so they follow his lead.

Simon notices his sister is on the verge of tears. "In a way," he says to her," it's a perfect ending."

"How so?" Helen asks.

"Saint Anthony's sanctuary wasn't abandoned; it was overrun by all that was bad in the world."

"It's not the time, Simon. Just try to be normal for once. Please."

Tarik interjects, "You aren't Simon Perenna, by any chance?"

"Why?"

"My condolences, for your parents."

"What?"

"I know it's late. The incident happened," he pauses to reflect, "around six months ago. I didn't know them but I served with a member of their security detail. He passed away too."

"I'm sorry, you must be mistaken."

Tarik looks at Simon, judging how to respond. "Yes, I must be mistaken," he finally says.

Simon glances at his sister. Her expression has not changed, though her hands are trembling slightly. He had not looked at her hands before however, so is unsure whether this is a new symptom.

When enough of the exhibit has been cleaned up to leave room for the forklift to put the crate in the centre of the room and then disengage the fork, the crew does so with exaggerated care. Then they accelerate, driving the lift back into the truck, stacking the rails, closing it up, having a final word with Tarik and driving off. Only the men in overcoats remain.

With the room largely cleared out, Tarik is able to take Tony to the side. He introduces him to one of the men, Joe, and explains United Monolith is to provide security for the museum while the object in the crate is on-site.

"What's in the crate?" Tony asks.

"Not for me to say," Tarik replies. "Your boss will tell you soon enough."

Tony does not argue. "The rest of you can go, then? You've certainly managed to add something special to the evening."

"Yes. After we take one more look around and replace the lock on the gate."

"Fine."

"Here's my card, just in case."

"Thanks."

The group takes the boxes to the basement. By the time they

are done, Tarik and the other suits are gone. They look for Joe, see he is on the bench out front, smoking and decide it will be better if they avoid interacting with him. They settle in the mauve corner and process what just happened. Pris and Max bring several bottles over and make sure everyone has a drink.

"Anna's gone," Helen observes with alarm.

"True," Simon says.

"You're not worried?"

"Nah, she'll be fine. It's a school night, so it was about time she took off."

"Right after she learned her parents were dead?"

"Nothing's confirmed. I wouldn't jump to conclusions. Anyway, she's got a good head on her shoulders. She'll be fine."

"If you say so."

"So, about the crate in the room," Saul says. "I suppose we shouldn't open it."

"Curious?" Max asks.

"Of course."

"Me too."

"Me three," Pris adds. The others, save Helen and Tony, follow suit.

"Give me her number," Helen orders Simon. "I just want to send her a quick text, make sure she's okay."

"Let's give her some space," Simon replies. "If she's not home when we get there, we can start to worry."

"So, about the crate in the room," Saul says.

"Stop it," Tony interrupts him.

"I guess maybe the museum is not going to close," Pris suggests.

"Tony can keep being a hermit," Simon says. "Is the security guard going to be a permanent fixture?"

"That's the impression I got from Tarik," Tony responds.

"I guess you can still be a hermit if he stays outside."

"We'll have to get you a new pig," Alex says.

"It's not really my sanctuary anymore," Tony points out.

"Depends on what's in the crate," Saul argues. "Maybe it's an artichoke you."

"I just don't understand how you can be so calm about the possibility that your parents are gone," Helen addresses Simon. "Unless you already knew?"

"First time I've heard of it. I guess I've taught myself not to worry about them. They've been in dangerous situations fairly regularly for as long as I can remember. Sure, they were around more in the beginning—Anna lost out on that, though I'm not sure that's a bad thing—but they were still gone most of the time.

"It all crystallized when I read Flaubert's The Temptation of Saint Anthony, as odd as that sounds. Some of you have already heard this; I apologize in advance. At one point, the devil flies Tony up to the heavens to demonstrate to him there are no heavens, religiously speaking. All there are are stars and planets and asteroids and meteoroids. They are incredible objects, but they aren't divine. Flaubert uses the word 'aeroliths' to describe them. It was the first time I had heard the word used outside my parent's company, Consolidated Aerolithics.

"I was in high school then, already questioning my parent's authority for some time. It was at that moment I realized they had in a way renounced their parental aura—that infallibility children imprint on those who give them life. They saw a choice between the parent myth and these celestial objects and decided to abandon the myth. I don't fault them for it; the myth was, well, a myth. Only, a lot of parents find a middle ground. Mine decided to go for the extreme, giving up any pretense of shepherding their offspring toward adulthood and independence.

"It's all a bit long-winded and metaphoric. The devil probably wasn't involved. Still, a whole bunch of people die in the centre of Africa on a regular basis. Why should I feel especially connected to a couple of them who have become no more than my faceless corporate benefactors? They're not even that but let's be generous. On the flip-side, why should I believe a thug from a competing corporation when the bills are still being paid?"

"The devil was definitely involved," Saul says. "Otherwise, your story is just weak sauce. A sad and sappy orphan story, only without the heart-wrenching poverty and red hair."

"To be clear, are you saying the red hair is heart-wrenching?" Alex asks.

"I'm saying we should open the crate to distract ourselves from Simon's sob story."

"You don't let go, do you?" Tony observes.

"It could be an artichoke you. How can you turn down the chance to find out?"

"It's not an artichoke me. It's some narcissistic commission from a company incapable of differentiating between corporate interest and public good."

"Oh, that was good."

"Is anger a vice?" Max asks.

"Given what's happened tonight, I don't think it matters," Pris replies.

"But for the record," Alex adds, "yes."

"Maybe it's a pig," Max suggests.

"A golden pig, to lead you astray," Saul adds.

"Now I'm thinking of the Arc of the Covenant and melting faces," Pris says.

"The faces only melted when the arc was opened. But the Nazi symbols were magically burnt off the crate."

The group turns to look at the crate. A United Monolith symbol is clearly stamped on the side facing them.

"Either that's not the Arc of the Covenant or United Monolith is not as evil as Nazis," Max concludes.

"The crate looks more like a monolith than the building," Alex notes. "If there's an actual monolith inside, I think I'd be disappointed."

"Depends if there's interesting script engraved on it," Pris says.

"That's true. Before it was frowned upon, corporations bought antiquities all the time."

Simon belatedly notices Helen has withdrawn from the conversation.

"I really appreciate your concern," he says to her, pulling out his phone. "I'm sorry if it seemed I was making light of the situation. Here's Anna's number."

Helen does not warm to his words, but manages to say, "We should give Anna some space, give her some time to work through it. We're not her parents. I'm not related at all."

"You're important to both of us. Blood doesn't mean anything, caring as much as you do does."

Helen nods, unconvinced.

"Fine," Tony concedes. "I will not be a part of opening the crate. In fact, I feel like joining Joe outside for a smoke. You all seem easily amused and prone to flights of devilish fancy. There are some tools in the basement you might be amused by."

"Wow," Saul says. "That was a whole lot of unnecessary verbal gymnastics. You are not responsible for our actions. Good, fine, make sure Joe doesn't come in. We're all on board."

"Yeah," Alex echoes. "Wow."

Tony exits through the red door. Saul disappears downstairs. Alex examines the crate, noting it is screwed together. Saul reappears with a couple pry bars.

"Not all cases are put together like in the movies," Alex tells him. "A drill with a Phillips bit would be ideal."

Saul curses, redescends and resurfaces with the tool. Alex takes it and goes to work on the front panel. Pris selects music to better cover the noise. Once the panel is loose, Max and Saul lower it and carry it off to the side. Everyone peers inside.

"It's a shield, right?" Saul asks.

"Yeah," Pris confirms. "A giant, golden shield."

"Is that real gold?" Max wonders.

"No idea. If it is, that would explain the security."

"It's like the shield from a coat of arms," Simon observes, "only blank. You'd think there'd be at least a 'UM' on it."

"Just because it was delivered by United Monolith," Alex argues, "doesn't mean they made it. It doesn't look very old though, and it seems like just the thing they might create to symbolize their place in the supposed Neolithic Era. Nothing like a metal sculpture to make it obvious nobody paid attention to the fact that the metal ages came after the Stone Age."

"I would have imagined a spear; something more aggressive," Saul comments.

"It needs a card to explain it," Helen says. "Especially now it's in a museum."

"Let's get the other panels off," Alex proposes, not waiting for a response before starting on one of the side panels. Ten minutes later, only the bottom of the crate is left with the sculpture. No one suggests trying to lift the piece to remove it.

The light reflecting off the polished surface makes the room noticeably brighter, banishing shadows to behind the curtains. For the second time this evening, the group pauses, trying to process what they are seeing.

"It is imposing," Max offers.

"It's like purified greed masquerading as society's protector," Pris says.

"Temptation doesn't get much more blatant," Simon observes.

"But our faces haven't melted off," Saul concludes, "so all's well that ends well."

Simon receives a text message from Yi-Fu letting him know Anna is at their place. He shows the message to Helen and echoes Saul: "All's well that ends well."

6

Anna has no desire to interact with Simon's friends, so she makes herself a spot by the artichokes with a blanket and pillows. She would have preferred the mauve corner but everyone else seems mysteriously attracted to it. The corner was never much help anyway, even though it was not entirely its fault. With her, it did not have much to work with. The artichokes have an affinity with fish-jesus, so they might do more to spark her imagination. They are Tony's totems, yet are also communal. The museum, at least in its artichoke identity, seems like a squat at odds with the rest of the neighbourhood.

She opens her notebook on her lap to the page with The Ear Stone Chronicles written across the top. Her eyes play across the artichoke table. The real thing has a natural symmetry, perhaps a certain beauty to the human eye. Chodkiewicz could probably distill it into a series of mathematical rules. He would probably call most pieces in front of her ugly, lacking proportionality and a bunch of other insults. Perhaps one or two have drawn out the natural beauty of the plant that inspired them. Another couple might have managed to blend in other rules, resulting in a symmetry all their own. She looks for the ones, particularly among the artichokes-as-flower, she would consider both deformed and beautiful.

"Can I join you?"

Anna looks up to see Helen standing over her. She quickly closes her notebook, then nods. As far as she is concerned, Helen is okay and there is no point being disagreeable. The chances of her making any progress are almost nil in any case. Helen rearranges some pillows and sits down beside her.

"Simon mentioned you come here pretty often," Helen says.

"Surget wanted evidence I was giving back to the community. This was the least bad option."

"You pitch in before school too?"

"No, that's different. Just a place to come to do homework."

"With a friend?"

"Sometimes."

"Why didn't you invite them tonight?"

"Oh, if I invited Nadia, she would have wanted to bring Martin. That would have led to more people coming and this place would end up being overrun by high schoolers. Nobody wants that."

"Ah. Wise. Rumour has it the museum is going to be closed."

"Tony says the City has been looking for an excuse to close it for years."

"If it does, what do you plan to do?"

"Dunno. The neighbourhood is just a series of boxes from the Monolith down. The museum is a box too but it has, I don't know, more substance to it or something."

"The other boxes are made out of ticky tacky?"

"I don't get it."

Helen pulls out her phone, finds the song "Little Boxes" and plays it for Anna.

"Yes, it's just like that. Only our boxes aren't that colourful. Until I move away, there aren't many options. Even then, I'll probably go to university. If the song's right, it'll be more of the same."

"Do you think Simon's made out of ticky tacky?"

"No, but he's Simon. He's always been a bit odd. He's got a sort of twisted imagination. Not all of us have that."

"What about The Ear Stone Chronicles? That seems pretty imaginative."

Anna frowns.

"Sorry, I saw it as you were closing your book. It's none of my business."

The conversation lapses into silence. Anna debates whether to respond and, if so, what she could possibly say about a couple scraggly ideas dying in the desert of the blank page.

"There's nothing to say. It's a title without a story."

"I bet there's a story behind the title."

"So? It's a not so clever play on music in our Neolithic Age. Animals can hear because they have small calcium deposits vibrating in their heads. The end." Anna suddenly wishes Nadia was there. Nadia would riff off the idea and lighten the mood. Then she would lose interest and randomly switch directions, pull out her phone or nod off. Helen is far too earnest.

"It could be something to build off. Or fish-jesus. They both pique my interest."

"Simon mentioned fish-jesus?"

"That's linked to music too, isn't it?"

"Fish-jesus isn't even my idea."

"Kristin Hersh, no?"

"It was something in a squat she stayed in sometimes when she was just starting out."

"I don't know much about her. I get the impression her music is intensely personal. Is that right?"

"I guess."

"In the seventies and early eighties, art school was all about grooming the next genius artist—someone whose ideas were unimaginably new and original. Students had their own studios with lockable doors. Visiting other studios was just not done, as other students' work could contaminate original lines of thought or dull individual brilliance. And that's not even taking into account the fear of having ideas stolen. Competition was fierce, as getting there—wherever there happened to be—first was pretty much all that counted.

"Kids formed bands as an act of rebellion. Most of them weren't musicians but that didn't matter. Being the best didn't matter. They were in it to create something as a group."

"You're saying I should join a band?" Anna runs through the

group decisions she followed leading her to break the school window.

"There are a lot of reasons to get involved in music and not all of them put music or creativity front and centre. That was my point."

"So I don't need an alien pen?"

"It's my turn to say I don't know what that means."

"Shakespeare's muse."

"I'm sure an alien pen can't hurt, short of it actually being a pen from another planet bent on world domination. Only, I don't think it's necessary. You should chase after your fish-jesus if that works for you but, just because it was important for Hersh, doesn't mean it's the only path to follow."

"It wasn't that important for her. It was more of an amusing anecdote."

"Well, there we are. And your brother would be the first to tell you he's not all that original. He just happens to dig up a lot of obscure and amusing trivia in his research."

"And turns them into day calendars."

"Day calendars?"

Anna tells Helen about the Day Calendar of Learned Heresies she keeps in her locker at school. The two go on to list interesting things Simon has come up with of late. Every one is based on eighteenth to nineteenth century French literature, the history of heretical Christian ideas or some mix of the two. Tarik enters as they conclude that Simon has his own box, even if neither he nor it is made of ticky tacky.

The music is lowered, the mood broken. A rumour rapidly circulates that the newcomer is United Monolith security. Helen asks if this is an ordinary occurrence.

"I've never seen any sort of security here before," Anna replies.

The crowd shifts toward the mauve corner to find out what is happening. Then, after a while, people start to leave. Helen and Anna stay where they are, figuring they will hear the news soon enough. Pris breaks off from the group, packing up the now superfluous seating. She drops by with some pillows to add to their area. Helen asks what is going on. Pris tells her about the delivery and Tony's reaction to it.

They follow Tarik with their eyes as he walks to the back and opens the door. Anna is hit by cold air when the museum's warmth escapes into the darkness. Tarik already appeared to her like a violation of the museum, an imposition of the neighbourhood's force under the watchful eye of the Monolith. The sanctity of the space was holding though, until now.

She had never questioned Tony's control. The museum could be shut down or transformed into something else, but not while the sign outside said Museum of Artichoke; not when Artie the Artichoke was fixed in his heroic pose and Tony was in the room. The two realities just could not exist at the same time. Yet this Uni-lith hoodlum has opened a massive breach and now has been joined by an invading force. Their vessel has accosted the museum and no one has what it takes to repel it.

The future suddenly seems bleak, hopeless. Feeling the urge to curl up and cry, Anna blindly feels around her mind for some support. Theodore of Byzantium is the only idea within reach. She repeats courage is overrated, heroism is overrated, dying gruesomely is overrated over and over like a mantra. Then she sees people packing up the artichokes, trying to save them. She joins in with feverish, clumsy movements, her mantra continuing its loop.

When the artichoke-as-flower falls off the table, she does not know if she is responsible. All she manages to do is cry out unintelligibly and gesture vaguely in its direction. It keeps its form after hitting the concrete; a radially symmetric cluster of flowers passing from French mauve to deep ultramarine, encircled by overlapping scales of buds. Under ordinary circumstances she may have wondered if it was any more interesting than a common silk plant, replicating nature without adding anything to it. It rolls smoothly away despite the bulging scales, instilling in her a certain admiration. Her twitchy movements and desire to shut down feel to her like a deformity, like she failed to stick another landing and is once again barely hobbling along.

Her eyes move up at the last minute, vaguely registering the menace of the forklift. A moment later, the artichoke is no more. Any notion of symmetry and elegant movement is crushed. It all seems inevitable. As if to confirm this conclusion, she hears her brother say: "In a way, it's a perfect ending." She redoubles her efforts to keep going, packing the other artichokes so no more meet the fate of the flower, all the while repeating her mantra. By the time she learns her parents are probably dead, she has no emotional room to process the news.

When no more objects are directly in front of her, she walks away. She goes through the red door, past the empty bench to the sidewalk and heads south along the main street. The sidewalk is mostly empty this late in the evening. A trickle of cars, of red and white lights, streams past. Light flows from the warmth of still-open businesses, over the sills of display windows and into the street. Most people she passes are on the other side of panes of glass, bathed in the heat the light left behind. Besides the occasional proposition and crude comment from smokers milling in front of the handful of bars on the strip, she is left alone with her thoughts.

The ground drops off at the south end of the neighbourhood. A promenade with a row of benches lines the crest. Despite the cool night made colder by the exposed edge, a variety of people; young couples, seniors, transients; take advantage of the seating. The conversations do not rise above a murmur and are quickly lost in the dark emptiness of the valley. Anna mentally throws her mantra over the edge, then collapses on an empty bench. It does not register that Adam is sitting three benches further along.

She wills her tears to come. Nothing happens; they seem to have dried up inside her, leaving a residue of helplessness and loss. She replays the forklift crushing the flower over the blackness in front of her. Then she searches for memories of her parents. The first thing that appears is the pictures of them in the house. Every one is a family photo of some sort, most taken in the midst of some group activity, filled with spontaneous smiles and charming goofiness. Passing through the frames, she finds her memories are not cohesive experiences but short sequences of movement tied to the captured moments. Her parents are likely gone forever and she feels more strongly about the loss of an ersatz artichoke flower.

The edge is right in front of her, the blackness a railing away. Why project memories onto it when she can be a part of it? She can imagine the jump, the fall, but not the landing. She might pass out beforehand or blink out right at impact. Or, still somehow be conscious, in shock, her mind blocking all unnecessary sensations, implementing all the heroic measures in its arsenal in a desperate, final struggle to survive.

None of it matters. She knows she will never cross beyond the protective barrier. All her talk about uncontrollable, scary imagination, about risks; none of it is real. She knows she cannot stick the landing. If she jumped, she would end up living a long life as a paraplegic. If she ever managed to write The Ear Stone Chronicles, it would end up being just imaginative enough to be off-putting but not enough to be truly superb. Her parents had leapt—there is no question in her mind why they had to leave her behind.

She abruptly gets up and heads back into the checkerboard. Making her way through the squares, she finds herself in front of Nadia's building. Yi-Fu picks up and buzzes her in as soon as he hears her voice. He greets her at the door.

"Nadia's asleep," he informs her.

"I'm actually here to talk to Sara."

"Ah, in that case, she's at the kitchen table."

He motions her in. She bends down to take off her shoes, pausing only for a moment when she sees slippers unevenly darkened by outside dirt and moisture on her feet. Then she goes into the kitchen. Sara is in the middle of scoring a proposal, surrounded by neat stacks of other contenders.

"Hi, Anna," she says without looking up. "Take a seat if you'd like. I'll only be a minute."

"Either of you need anything?" Yi-Fu asks. Both Sara and Anna shake their heads, so he retreats to a comfortable chair and a book.

Once Sara has finished scribbling a note in a box of the scoring sheet, she glances at the clock on the wall and then focuses on Anna.

"It's a bit late, isn't it?" she asks. "Is everything okay?"

"Did you know my parents are dead?" Anna asks evenly.

Sara is taken aback. "I... what?"

Anna repeats the question.

"No. Wow, that's awful, when did this happen?"

"Six months ago, apparently."

"Six months ago?" Sara thinks back to what was going on half a year before. End of year budgeting and project reviews are all that come to mind. "I'm really sorry, Anna. I don't know anything about it."

Silence fills the room. Anna looks intensely at her friend's mother. Sara takes in Anna's reddened eyes and disheveled hair. Yi-Fu listens in discreetly.

"Why do you think I would know about your parents?" Sara finally asks.

"Doesn't everybody at United Monolith know?" Anna starts to raise her voice.

"What exactly are you referring to?"

"Did you know about the attack on the museum tonight?"

"We can discuss this calmly but you are going to have to give me more details. Can we start with which museum you are talking about?"

"Are you saying you don't know about United Monolith security overrunning the museum tonight?"

It dawns on Sara that Anna could be talking about the delivery Driss Rehg had spoken of that morning, a delivery she was supposed to manage but had completely forgotten about. It was a valuable item, so of course there would be security.

"I am aware of a delivery. Was a package dropped off?"

"'A package dropped off?'" Anna starts laughing.

"I will look into it in the morning," Sara says, suddenly very tired. "If there were problems, they will be dealt with."

"The art destroyed?" Anna's voice cracks; the nervous energy keeping her going starts to dissipate.

"If anything was damaged, we will work out compensation." Sara pauses, before tacking on, "How is this related to your parents?"

Anna does not respond. Sara puts two and two together: someone involved in the delivery said something. The timeline starts to resonate. Rehg had said the breakthrough in negotiations to buy Consolidated Aerolithics happened six months ago. He had also said the Perennas would head the new space mining division. There was no hint of them being gone but they had always fought to keep their independence. Regardless, it is not something she can deal with tonight.

"Do you know the name of the person who told you?" Sara asks.

"Terry maybe…"

"Tarik? Tarik Williams?"

Anna nods, deflated.

"I will talk to him tomorrow. We will get to the bottom of this, I promise. Do you want to stay here tonight?"

"I sent a message to your brother," Yi-Fu says," so he won't be worried."

"No," Anna replies.

"Let me drive you home then."

"No."

Anna gets up to leave. Yi-Fu and Sara look at each other as if to decide whether they should insist. They choose not to. Sara approaches Anna and hugs her, saying, "We'll figure this out." Anna does not respond to the warmth but does not pull away. Then, feet once more in sullied slippers, she is out the door.

7

"Kiddo!" Yi-Fu calls through the door. "You're going to be late for school!"

Nadia looks groggily at her phone until the meaning of the numbers registers. "Shit," she mumbles, sitting up. She does the bare minimum to be presentable enough to face the world. As she slips on her shoes, her father comes to the entrance and leans against the wall, his favourite coffee cup in hand.

"Thought you were getting up early these days."

"Only when Anna texts me, usually several times." She decides to double check her phone, finding a couple unread messages from the night before from several people, including a non-apology from Martin, but nothing from Anna. "No messages from her."

"Not surprising. She had a late night last night."

"How do you know?"

"She came here, to talk to your mother. We decided not to wake you."

Nadia stops, her attention captured. "That's really weird. What about?"

"You should ask her yourself."

"Not even a hint?"

"It's something she would want to tell you directly."

"But it wasn't important enough to wake me up last night?"

"It wasn't something that pressing. That being said, I will understand if you want to put off going skiing."

"You're killing me."

"Have a lovely day at school!" He walks back into the apartment.

Despite the lateness, Nadia stops by the museum on the way to school. She slows when she sees a Uni-lith security guard sitting on the bench out front instead of Adam. They exchange a curt nod as she goes up to the red door. Inside, an ambiguously grey Tony is on a ladder, busy taking down the curtains. No sign of festivities or artichokes remains. The shield dominates the room, multiplying the brightness of the light from the skylight and forcing Nadia to squint. After a second, she bursts out laughing.

Tony looks at her, a question written on his face.

"It's absolutely perfect. I have to take a picture—I can take a picture, right?"

He nods and she circles the sculpture, taking multiple shots and a short video.

"You don't know Mr. Chodkiewicz, do you?" she asks as she circles.

He shakes his head, then realizes she isn't looking at him and says, "No."

"Then you won't get it. But it's perfect; so, so bad." Suddenly, she remembers why she is there. "Anna didn't come in this morning?"

"No."

"Ah. Well, thanks! I have to go. I'm already late for school."

She is gone a moment later, a skip in her step. Back in the street, she breaks into an easy jog. A block from the collection of boxes, she runs into a dour-looking Anna.

"Did you know there's a giant golden shield in the museum?" she blurts out excitedly, showing Anna the video.

"Figures," Anna replies without enthusiasm, barely glancing at Nadia's phone.

"'Figures'? You must know something I don't know. But, who cares? It's brilliant, literally, and perfect in the most horrible way."

"What are you talking about?"

"Mr. Chodkiewicz! His uselessness is ugliness rant! Only his best deranged harangue ever! I will never forgive myself for not recording it."

"I don't remember."

"Of course you do. The example he went on about was a golden shield. He compared it to all sorts of math theories accepted because they were beautiful or elegant or whatever when in reality they were grotesque. Then he did this whole detour on women's bodies only being beautiful because they were commodified, which led into this whole thing about the socially acceptable prostitution all the girls prettying themselves up instead of studying were buying into. He actually looked at all of us with his creepy eyes when he asked if we all wanted to be prostitutes when we grew up. You could tell the desire to say 'whores' was ready to burst out of him, making his eyes extra buggy. It was epic!"

Anna shrugs. They enter the empty hallway of the school and go straight to Anna's locker. Nadia does not care to drop off her jacket, just go to class. She is content however to dwell on the morning's unexpected developments and wait for Anna before facing fifty minutes—or however much time is left—of Elizabethan poetry.

"Tony needs to change the sign to Museum of Ugliness," Nadia muses. "Or maybe not. We need to record people's reactions. Anyone who doesn't get the repugnance of it all needs to be sent to some sort of re-education camp. You know, I was worried about today, what with you not texting and that security lady on Adam's bench, but it's all worth it. Got to sleep in, epic ugliness...and the day's young! Today's heresy had better keep things going, is all I'm saying."

Anna grabs the calendar and flips through it.

"That's no fun," Nadia complains. "You're ruining the surprise!"

Sabellius, Audius, Tertullien, Helvidius, Jovinien, Marcel are passed by, followed by several Gnostic sects. Anna pauses at the Ophites and Cainites, tearing off the pages and stuffing them into a pocket, then puts the calendar back.

"First cheating, now no heretical amusement, misplaced quips, excommunicable sarcasm," Nadia sighs as she follows Anna to class. "Not even any appreciation for my wording. That's what really breaks my heart. First there was Adam not being on his bench—but

I told myself he was yesterday's heresy—and then this. I might just have to write a wistful sonnet about it."

They open the door to their English class. The group is quiet, working on their poems.

"Well, look who decided to show up," Mrs. Sobeski says dryly, getting up from her desk and meeting them at the door. "Out." She leads them back into the hallway to have a conversation without disturbing the other students. Once the door is closed, she asks, "Give me a reason I shouldn't assign you detention and make-up work to be finished before you can rejoin the class. You can't blame Mr. Surget this time."

Shit, Nadia says to herself. In the midst of her golden-shield euphoria, it completely slipped her mind she would need a reason, other than the actual truth of sleeping in, for being late.

"My parents are dead," Anna states lifelessly.

"What?!" Nadia blurts out.

Sobeski narrows her eyes, trying to judge whether Anna is telling the truth.

"Is that why you were at my place last night?" Nadia continues, "But why? What do my parents have to do with it? How did it happen? Are you okay?"

"You should see Mr. Surget," Sobeski interrupts Nadia's flow of questions. Truth or lie, a student saying their parents are dead justifies a trip to the counselor.

"I should go too, right?" Nadia says. "She really needs support."

"Fine," Sobeski states in a way that makes it clear she does not want this to be her problem.

Anna hands Sobeski the one-pager on Shakespeare's muse and walks away, toward Surget's office. Nadia tails her. Once they have turned a couple corners and find themselves close to an exit, Nadia grabs her friend's arm and pulls her out of the school.

"But Surget," Anna complains listlessly.

"Screw him." They take a line away from the collection of boxes hidden from anyone who might look out a window. Nadia stops at the edge of the grounds and faces Anna.

"Is it true? I mean I totally get you saying that to get out of detention and everything—it's not as if your parents are ever around—but I need to know."

"They might be gone."

"Oookay."

"I don't know. Some Uni-lith security thug gave us—mainly Simon, really—his condolences last night."

"Weird! Like, he came to your house?"

"At the museum."

"Ah, everything is starting to come together. So, you asked my mom about it?"

Anna nods.

"And that stupid shield is connected?"

Anna nods again.

"This morning is full of surprises. What did my mom say?"

"She'd look into it today."

"Yeah, well, she'll do it but that doesn't mean you'll know the truth."

"What do you mean?"

"She tries, you know, to keep her humanity and all. But she's Uni-lith through and through. If the company's involved, she'll cover it up. Short of them literally pulling the trigger, anyway."

"You really think so?"

"I guess we'll see. So, how do you want to celebrate your freedom? After having your parents constantly on your back, you can finally stand up straight!"

Anna shakes her head.

"Sorry. It's gotta suck."

"No, it's alright. One of us has to lighten the mood. You're doing all the heavy lifting."

"Well, so long as it's appreciated. Seriously though, my plan went as far as getting out of the school. Now we're on our own." They walk further into the checkerboard.

"So it's a golden shield?"

"Weren't you there?"

"I left before the crate was opened."

"Yeah. I almost want to go back to school to show the video to Chodkiewicz, just to see his reaction. He'd probably say something predictable and condescending though. Like I found it because I have some affinity with it, the resemblance is striking save, of course, that the shield has more perfect symmetry. Or I did the right thing in bringing it to him so he can mansplain it to me but good on me for kind of understanding. Maybe it's a woman's intuition thing. His rants are great, but not when you are in the crosshairs and within spitting distance. Ech."

"I really need to cry."

"Right now? I can pull over, though you really should have done that before we left."

"Also, blowing up the Monolith would feel pretty good."

"With or without people inside? It is a pretty high-profile target, at least for the neighbourhood. Without people in it though, right?"

"Yeah, don't want to kill anyone. Except maybe the CEO and the head of security."

"Just don't say any of that online. Also, lacks imagination. And, the big boss here is my mom. The CEO just came through town but is already gone. Nothing all that important is done here anymore. Some interesting science; that's about it."

"They came into the museum last night as if they owned the place. The whole neighbourhood isn't all that different. It would probably be Uni-lith security rather than the police knocking down my door if I posted threats."

"That sounds a bit dystopian."

"Private security keeping people down has a long and storied history. Tony goes on about how Uni-lith bought up and razed the neighbourhood with the mayor's blessing. There was apparently even a big press conference where they announced the billions of dollars in private investment, as if there was no downside. The museum picked up the scraps of what was there before. And now Uni-lith has taken that over too."

"At least now you're talking! Not that I want a reputation for defending the Monolith but doesn't the City constantly threaten to close the museum? What if the ugly shield is the only thing keeping it open? I'm sorry but what was left isn't all that interesting."

"It's not that the shield is there. It's how they brought it in. They bulldoze and steamroll and maybe even kill. Why wouldn't they kill to get their hands on the cobalt mines and whatever else my parent's company has? It's all about not caring who they hurt."

"I know a perfect place! Can't believe I didn't think of it before." Nadia leads Anna across several blocks and then between two apartments. The walls are covered with lines, patterns and Saint Glinglin verses twisted into complex arabesques of white and gold on a constantly shifting blue background. Despite being painted, the ensemble has the appearance of carefully arranged tiles. Cheap-looking café chairs are scattered, empty, through the space.

"Somewhere in the graffiti there's an explanation," Nadia says, walking from one end to the other before giving up, "but I can never find it. It's inspired by some necropolis in Uzbekistan, if I recall correctly. Somewhere in Central Asia, at least. Definitely a necropolis. I love the word 'necropolis,' but not in a morbid way."

Anna walks the length of the walls, running her fingers across the paint. She then sits and gazes at them from a distance. "It's aged perfectly. You'd think it was a thousand years old. The gold seems... but that's probably accurate too. How do you always know where these places are?"

"I have an intimate connection to Saint Glinglin. Or, they keep moving the bouldering walls but are nice enough to send me a new map when they do."

"Right, your boulderless bouldering."

"You've spent too much time around my dad."

"But a necropolis?"

"People should have a place to grieve."

"But why Uzbekistanian, if that's the word?"

"No idea. Does it matter?"

"I'm not sure people would understand it."

"But it sure is impressive."

Anna soon finds herself lost in the intricate patterns. Nadia answers the more important messages on her phone. She also texts her dad to ask whether the death of Anna's parents was the extent of the news he would not tell her that morning and to let him know she skipped out on class to help Anna cope. She finishes by saying she loves him. Anna's parents have almost always been absent, so them being gone changes nothing for everyday life. She is scared to imagine how her life would change if her parents disappeared all of a sudden.

"Why do the Saint Glinglin followers move the murals?"

"They don't like permanence; something about accumulating power and authority, which ends up being accepted more because it's there than because it makes sense."

"Not because of Uni-lith rules or anti-graffiti laws or anything like that?"

"I don't think so. They're against the Monolith as far as I know, though it's more of a philosophical disagreement. Honestly, I barely talk to them. I'm not the best person to ask."

The two stare at the walls for a while.

"Helen thinks I should form a band," Anna says.

"Who's Helen?"

"My brother's girlfriend. She thinks the whole fish-jesus thing is too personal; too intense."

"She's not wrong. It does come off as pretty intense, with a healthy dose of weird. Even as a totem. Are you going to do it?"

"Dunno."

"You don't play an instrument but you could learn. There's a ton of bands started before the members knew how to play. It could be fun. You could even name it The Ear Stone Chronicles. Or maybe that would be the title for the first album."

"You wouldn't want to join?"

"I already have too much stuff going on. But I'd come to all your shows. And you can always use me as a sounding board for your lyrics."

"I'm useless at writing."

"You might find poetry easier than a script. Hey, Martin wants to join us for lunch. Would that be okay?"

Anna frowns but nods.

"Thanks! You're the best. Maybe some of the gang would be interested in your band."

"Please don't say anything."

"No worries, I won't." Nadia realizes at that moment how right her father was that morning to insist some things were not his to say. Luckily, the ugly shield should give her more than enough to talk about. The monstrosity might even give Martin a new obsession, saving the world from yet another sketch of the Monolith.

8

Sara pulls into the parking lot behind the museum in a metallic green wagon, the repacked box of proposals in the seat beside her. The car is both darker and shinier than Tony's Accord, the only other car there. Before exiting her vehicle, she takes in the fencing and the shiny new lock on the gate, concluding she will have to go around the block to enter the building. How convenient, she thinks to herself. Walking back to the alley, she notices someone in a car in the facing lot looking at her but dismisses it.

She reads the sign as she passes, Museum of Artifice, then stops in front of the bench where the United Monolith security guard is sitting.

"Museum of Artifice?" She asks.

The guard, Selena, shrugs.

"Shouldn't you be stationed inside, with eyes on the shield?"

"I'm where I should be, ma'am."

"If you say so." Sara makes a mental note to bring it up at her meeting with Tarik this afternoon.

The shield glows in the morning light, giving the impression it is a source of luminescence unto itself. Sara pauses, taken aback. She expected it to be the size of a regular shield, at most that of the rectangular ones she imagines used by the Roman legions. She also expected it to be more ornate, which would have broken up the massive reflective surface and made it more, she searches for the word, artistic perhaps. After getting used to the shininess, she has to admit it is very plain; impressive only because it happens to be a significant amount of gold and not for any particular craftsmanship. Crude is how she would describe it, as if it was from the Paleolithic or Mesolithic Age.

She is startled when she notices an obstinately grey-looking figure standing beside her. It is as if he has an aura of dullness preventing the light from brightening his disposition.

"It is, in a way, an impressive piece," Tony opens.

"Arresting, yes, but after the first impression..."

"If only the zeitgeist hadn't dropped 'Neolithic' on us without a sense of how it was a departure from previous times."

"Exactly. The shield would, if memory serves, be neo-Meso or neo-Paleolithic, but we just jumped into neo-Neolithic. Putting aside of course that it is made of metal. I was just thinking that."

"It will all be sorted out in retrospect."

"Less marketing, more anthropology. Can't happen soon enough. I'm Sara Robin, from United Monolith. You must be Tony Abbott."

"Ah."

"I understand last night's delivery did not go well. I'm here to apologize for the logistical shortcomings and make arrangements for better collaboration moving forward."

"Without an appointment?"

"Frankly, Mr. Abbott, an understanding has already been established between the United Monolith Corporation and the City for the delivery of this artifact as a gesture of support for the museum. Due to its priceless nature, an agreement regarding security was also put into place. United Monolith reasonably expected City management to communicate these agreements to staff as needed, just as we did to our logistics and security personnel. The communications failure, and the issues of last night arising from it, reside fully with the City.

"In other words, Mr. Abbott, my apology to you is purely informal. Any arrangements with you will likewise be informal. It is in United Monolith's interest to ensure nothing happens that may cause the Corporation any embarrassment, regardless of where the fault may lie. For the moment, a direct line of communication with you is necessary.

"Formal negotiations will be beginning next week regarding the future of the museum. The decision as to your involvement is the purview of City management. Until they decide you are officially part of the discussion, there will be no appointments or other formalities. Does that make sense, Mr. Abbott?"

"Which leaves what, exactly?"

Sara hands Tony her card and checks the time on her phone. "A direct line to me."

Tony takes the card, glances at it, then puts it in a pocket.

Sara waits a moment for him to give her a card. When one is not forthcoming, she asks, "Do you have a card?"

"Nothing recent. One second." He takes one of the leftover brochures for the curtain exhibit, writes his coordinates on the back and gives it to her.

"Thank you. This is my first time in the museum. Do you want to show me around?" Sara starts walking around the room, so Tony follows her. She looks at the curtains that are still hanging.

"We are actually between exhibits."

"Are the curtains background or part of the exhibit?"

"They were the exhibit. Theatre curtains."

"Odd, without anything behind them."

"Actually, they were hung so we are behind them."

"We are the show?"

"In a manner of speaking."

"Can I touch them?"

Tony hands her a pair of gloves. "We control the temperature and humidity as best we can. With only one room and doors directly to the outside, that isn't saying much. Anything fragile or, at least until last night, particularly valuable is kept at the main municipal museum."

Sara pulls back a mauve curtain, exposing the bare wall behind. "It would be more interesting with a mirror or a picture of an audience."

Tony does not comment. The tour of the room quickly comes to an end. Sara takes a final look around and notices straps hanging from the skylight frame. She asks what they are for.

"You're only the second person who's noticed. For a short time, the building was a recital space cum piano bar. The room is pretty small, so they rigged up some pulleys and straps to lift the piano out of the way when not in use. Only, it blocked most of the natural light and having a piano hanging overhead was disconcerting, so it wasn't used much."

"The only thing worse would have been an anvil, no doubt. What was the building used for originally?"

"It was a power substation for the tramway line that used to run up and down the street."

"Must have been a long time ago."

"Pre-war, less than a century."

"What's the next exhibit?"

"Hinges."

Sara glances at the time. "I'd heard that. Are they special in any way?"

"No."

She imagines Rehg's reaction to the cohabitation of the one-of-a-kind golden shield with a bunch of fixtures that could be bought at any hardware store. "Then why show them?"

"They are the physical remnant of a story. They are valuable because of that connection. We can talk about the pre-war boom that generated the demand for them, their creation in eastern factories and the railway lines that brought them, along with most of the other manufactured goods at the time, to town. Then there's the whole architecture discussion, the craftsman and foursquare styles, and portraits of the sort of people who flocked to these new tramway neighbourhoods.

"It isn't all that different from arrowheads or pottery fragments, which typically aren't all that important in themselves. Also, if I may, it might be considered hypocritical for a representative of the company responsible for demolishing the houses and destroying everything special from the period to be critical about the quality of what is left."

"And also responsible for building desperately needed high-quality affordable housing? United Monolith doesn't hide from the difficult choices made in the past but insists the story is fair and balanced. I wouldn't call that hypocritical."

Selena pops her head in, looks around, then closes the door again.

"The first thing you could do is provide some history for the shield. As far as I know, it could have been cast yesterday."

"I'll see what I can do. From what I understand, there were some items damaged yesterday?"

"Only one directly, crushed under the forklift."

"Which implies indirect damage?"

"Through hasty packing to get everything out of the way."

"I see. Insurance?"

"None. Items here don't generally have much value, as I said earlier."

"What was the crushed item?"

"An artichoke flower. I have a picture of it downstairs, if you'd like to see it."

Sara looks at the time. "No, I have to go. Send me the details and an estimate. We can see what can be worked out."

"Don't worry about it. Thank you for dropping by."

They shake hands and Sara leaves. She dwells for an instant on the sort of person who would not be tempted by compensation offered by a company with deep pockets, who would admit nothing at the museum had any real value. The simple explanation is that he is a bureaucrat; capable in his narrow routine and uninterested in complicating his life by going beyond the well-defined limits of his role. It does not quite fit with his apparent independence, though his managers may have stuck him here with everything else they considered worthless to wile away the time before his retirement.

Then his position's empty box can be reallocated elsewhere in the corporation. The following budget will ask for a new box, essential for staffing the museum but not a high priority overall. Council will not fund it—one of many hard decisions to rein in spending and keep taxes at a reasonable level—, setting up the museum's closure due to lack of resources. Add to that the investment she saw in the papers recently to modernize the central museum and archives and a neat balance is struck between promoting municipal history and hard fiscal realities. Then United Monolith drops fifteen tonnes of gold in the middle of it. Just the sort of administrative scheming that makes her wish she never left the lab.

As soon as Sara arrives at the Monolith, she has to hurry, box in arms, to a long meeting of the committee struck to evaluate the proposals. The gathering is, predictably enough, held on the dark side of the building. Judgments ricochet between going through the motions and excessive nitpicking, but the momentum of the agenda carries through to the end. Immediately after, she makes her way to a meeting with Tarik on the bright side, leaving the box with Hassan.

Tarik is already in the room, a floor down from and practically identical to the one Rehg used as a temporary office yesterday. The head of security has a series of phones and other devices laid out on the table in a similar fashion to the CEO. Unlike the chief, Tarik is sitting at the table, relaxed but clearly ready to pick up one of the little black boxes in front of him and deal with any situation that might arise. The neighbourhood that so entranced Rehg seems to hold no interest for him.

On one hand, she is happy another barely coherent Beauty and the Beast monologue is evidently not in the cards. On the other, a meeting she has to lead without a well-defined objective or clear agenda always makes her uncomfortable. The thought of doing up an agenda had crossed her mind and then, like the delivery itself, got lost in the shuffle.

"Thank you for taking the time to meet with me," Sara says as she sits down and opens her laptop.

"Not a problem."

"So, the shield. What can you tell me about the delivery last night?"

"The order came down that it needed to be delivered. It was valuable, so a security escort was required during the delivery. In addition, a low-level presence had to be put in place and will be maintained for the duration of the item's stay off-site. Per procedure, security led the operation. From our perspective, it was a success."

"Is it normal for you to be involved directly?"

"I am not generally on the ground, no."

"Why were you in this case?"

"A request from Driss Rehg. The item is a seventeen point three tonne block of gold."

"We move larger quantities of far more valuable rare earth minerals all the time."

"Forgive my directness, but not to a glorified shack masquerading as a museum. Of course, Dr. Rehg did not express these specific concerns. It is my job to evaluate the risks."

"Can you go over the conflict with the people in the museum at the time of delivery?"

"When we arrived, a—I do not know how to describe it—an artichoke orgy or cult gathering was in progress. We informed them of the delivery. We delivered the item, set up the security detail and left."

"You seem to be leaving out some details."

"The group was not aware of the delivery, which under the circumstances came as no surprise. Some individuals contested it without the authority to do so. The group's confusion was managed and did not escalate into conflict, let alone violence. One artichoke sculpture—I am using the word liberally—of negligible value was damaged."

"You couldn't have held off on the delivery until the situation was calmer?"

"Continue to forgive me for my directness, but orders from Dr. Rehg do not come with additional funds. They are absorbed within the existing budget of the units involved. The guards and swampers were on the clock. We had clear orders and happened to run into an illicit artichoke orgy. The situation was managed without unnecessary expenditures. Second guessing comes dangerously close to implying I do not know how to do my job."

"No one took a video? Nothing on social media?"

"The only thing on social media is a video your daughter posted this morning." Tarik finds the video on one of his phones, then slides it across the table.

Sara is at first taken aback. She watches the video and is relieved to see it has nothing to do with the issues of last night. Reflecting, she realizes Nadia was at home at the time of the delivery.

"It lacks context perhaps," Tarik continues, "but is the sort of coverage I understand Dr. Rehg was hoping for. Something to raise the profile of the museum. Just don't look at the comments."

Sara instinctively looks at the comments. "It's a competition for the most creative way of saying the shield is hideous. I don't understand."

"It is best not to try. The point is last night's operation was both a success and, given the speed of news these days, ancient history. Does that suffice?"

"Thank you for going over this with me. I know you are a busy man. I have one more item. Did you happen to mention last night that the Perennas had passed away?"

Tarik does not respond immediately. "Yes. That was out of line."

"Why exactly? Have they died?"

"It was unprofessional. I can't say what happened to them."

"Are you saying you don't know or you just can't say?"

"I can't say. If that was the last question, I have other business to attend to."

"Of course, thank you again. How long are you going to be in town?"

Tarik starts packing up. "Until the next crisis takes me elsewhere. The joy of technology is you can work anywhere, until you can't."

Once Tarik has left, Sara stands where Rehg did a day before, a floor above. She looks over the checkerboard and the awkward pile of boxes. A quick and completely inconclusive response for Anna forms in her mind, is filed away and her thoughts turn to potential resolutions of the reduced neodymium magnet problem. The presentation yesterday went as well as could be hoped. Rehg seemed satisfied, for the moment. Without solid results however, the team likely will not be so fortunate next time.

9

Simon floats up to semi-consciousness as Helen gets out of bed. Her words, "I've got a class to teach," worm their way into his dream. The scene of him as an Indiana Jones-like archaeologist breaking into the government warehouse where the Arc of the Covenant ended up shifts. Instead of him being alone, stealthily bypassing security measures and armed guards in the dead of night, he is leading a tour of the facility for a noisy group of students. The warehouse is just as dingy but there is more light and the myriad crates suddenly have viewing windows. Everyone takes their turn at each window, like at an aquarium. Only, he can never get close enough to see inside. He keeps explaining, endlessly explaining, without ever being able to confirm if his words have any relation to whatever is in the boxes. It is a moot point however, as his students pay no attention to his words. They are only interested in whatever is behind the glass.

He drifts back up to the surface some time later. The bright light streaming in around the blinds persuades him to get up. After some coffee and toast, he faces a stack of papers he has been putting off grading for several days. At least they are for a British imperial history course, a subject he cares little about. The inevitable butchering of the material will leave him largely indifferent. The first page of the first paper makes him curious about the weather outside. He turns on his computer and checks the forecast. With the browser already open, it just makes sense to also look into what is going on in the world. An hour later, he rereads the first page of the first paper, which draws him to wonder if he should make some effort to find out if his parents are still alive.

The first call is to Consolidated Aerolithics. The company

has a sort of hotline for family members needing to get in contact with loved ones on assignment in hard-to-reach locales. Simon is convinced his parents could find an internet or phone connection somewhere if they really wanted to. Company policy however is to go through the glorified switchboard and, since they are the bosses, they were not inclined to buck the rules, at least for their children. Every time he has called, the person on the other end claims to be his parent's personal assistant. Given how many times the name has changed, all the while the script staying the same, he has his doubts.

This time is no different. He takes a certain pleasure in asking Tina how she likes working for dead people. He speculates that his parents are not much for micromanaging but that the lack of direction must get frustrating after a while. Tina assures him his parents, while unreachable at the moment, are very much alive. He asks for proof of life, imagining himself in the role of hostage negotiator. She laughs off his request, implies he is being overly dramatic and promises to have his parents call as soon as they have finished their inspection tour. She cannot provide an estimate for when that might be, as one might expect. He concludes she would make a very unprofessional kidnapper.

The next call is to the embassy in Kinshasa. When he gets through, his suspicion that the glorified hotline is nothing more than a ruse is reinforced. He starts by explaining that his parents are visiting the country and that he is worried because he has not heard from them in the past week. Saying there has been no direct communication for over a year would have probably seemed suspicious. The response is nobody by his parents' names has registered with the embassy. There have also been no recent incidents involving citizens of which the embassy is aware.

Simon asks if companies operating in the country are registered. It turns out they typically are and Consolidated Aerolithics is. Not only that, his parents are noted as officers of the company present in the Congo. It feels perfect; his parents do not exist as individuals but rather as arms of the corporation. They are not so much human as an economic-industrial construct. The notion of death has no real meaning for them. He is tempted to ask if there has been a bankruptcy or involuntary restructuring on record in the past year.

Instead, he waits for the bureaucrat to examine the files. He passes the time wondering how much this phone call is costing the company and, more conspiratorially, whether it is being flagged—maybe even bugged. It is difficult to imagine that changing anything. The obvious course for Consolidated Aerolithics, if they are involved, is to stonewall indefinitely, something they already seem to be doing. They might have to do more if he decides to fly to Africa and investigate personally, but what are the chances he would do that?

The voice on the other end of the line starts talking again. As if he is still asleep, Simon incorporates the words into his vision of the all-too-convenient mining accident that cuts his life and investigation short. He shakes his head and follows the voice back to reality. The bureaucrat informs him there have not been any incidents in the past year linked to the company. Most of the mines the company has an interest in are in Katanga however, which is not considered a secure zone. People investigating worker abuse and safety violations, especially regarding child labour, have disappeared. He will look into it further but under the circumstances cannot promise anything.

Simon provides his contact information, thanks the voice and hangs up. He considers going back to grading but gets sidetracked by his curiosity. Katanga, child labour and cobalt mining are far more interesting than what he is supposed to be doing. As they are linked to his parents' disappearance, he can also easily justify the digression. He is well down the rabbit hole when he hears the front door, a level down, open and close.

His mind immediately goes to the most poetically coincidental possibility of who might have entered: his parents. Then his mind fills with doubt. He concludes it is either Anna, somewhat out of character because of what happened last night, or Helen, because she forgot something. Either way, he does not want to be caught procrastinating and have to weather disparaging comments. He has after all only had one cup of coffee all day, so is not up to defending himself. Anna arrives at the top of the stairs as he finishes the second page of the first paper.

"What are you doing home?" Simon asks.

"Does it matter?" Anna falls into a chair. She drops her bag beside her, resulting in a muffled clanking of empty bottles.

Simon looks at the clock but does not trust it. He searches his immediate vicinity for his phone, finally seeing it on the kitchen counter. It is unclear how it managed to get all the way over there, way too far away to check the time without undue effort. "What time is it?"

"Lunchtime."

"I guess it doesn't matter then."

"The school didn't call?"

"Might have. Why?"

"I wasn't at school for very long this morning."

"Did you tell them?"

"About mom and dad? Yeah."

"Ah."

"They wanted me to see Surget. I couldn't handle more of him."

"Ah. Well, are you okay?"

"My parents just died."

"What a coincidence! Mine too! Only, I guess it was a while back. But nobody tells me anything."

"It's not funny."

"Humour is how I cope. I highly recommend it."

Anna does not reply.

"Seriously though, I did call Consolidated and the embassy in the Congo this morning."

"And?"

"Nothing. Sorry."

"Not your fault."

"You deserve an answer."

"Do I? After all the shit I said about them yesterday?"

"Don't beat yourself up about it. You were right and, in any case, it doesn't matter much now. The embassy is looking into it, so we might hear something yet."

Anna stays silent.

"Should I call the school?"

"Probably."

"I'll let them know you won't be in for the rest of the day." Simon goes to the kitchen and grabs his phone. He listens to the two messages waiting for him; one from Surget, the other from the principal. Both effectively assume Anna was lying without being so crass as to come out and say it. Both express grave concerns about her attitude, which need to be discussed. Instead of returning the calls, Simon phones the general office number and informs a secretary of Anna's absence.

He sits back down at the table and looks at his sister, who is staring off into space. "They don't seem to like you very much," he points out.

"Nope."

"Anything I should know?"

"Ever since the window, it's like I've been locked out of the anonymous middle. I'm trouble. Says so in my file. Must be true."

"Anything else?"

"Are you trying to be responsible now?"

"Don't want to be blindsided, is all."

"What do we do about our parents?"

"Wait, for now. Focus on other things for the time being. Don't let them drag us down, no matter what happens."

"If the company takes the house?"

"We'll figure it out, after the embassy does its thing." Simon begins to find the conversation more tedious than marking papers. It was kind of fun to investigate his parents' disappearance from the comfort of home. With his sister though, he has nothing to say to assuage her concern or guilt. There are no comforting answers or platitudes on offer. If it was not for the hostile messages, he would suggest she go back to school, if only as a distraction. Not knowing how to make a smooth transition, he exaggerates the movement of turning to the third page of the paper in front of him.

He is midway through the second paper when Anna speaks. "What do you know about Saint Glinglin?"

Resisting the temptation to restart the conversation, even if the subject is at first blush far more interesting, he slides his laptop over to her without a word. She takes it and searches for the expression.

"Blah, blah, experimental book written by Raymond Queneau, published originally in 1948, an attempt to create a modern religious story, Freudian, blah." Anna continues silently for a while, then resumes reading out loud. "Modern usage. Queneau's story included the double destruction of the father and the representation of the father by the son, followed by the son's self-sacrifice and deification, or quasi-deification. Queneau used the term 'negalith' to describe what the son aimed to accomplish. The term was a neologism and play on 'megalith,' another word for statue. The son wanted to replace the symbol of patriarchy with nothing. Despite this intention, he ended up replacing the father.

"The book was relatively obscure until a group of multinational corporations associated with rare and semi-rare earth elements combined their marketing efforts to promote the current age as the Neolithic Era. Resistance to this effort was inspired by the idea of the negalith. Most followers of Saint Glinglin minimize their use of products with rare and semi-rare earth components, such as blah, blah and cars. Others take a more symbolic approach, replacing stone with ephemeral constructions in a variety of applications, such as headstones, blah and blah.

"Certain radical groups aim to destroy the corporations, along with their permanent representations, as the patriarchal figures of the religion of late-stage capitalism. Blah, citation needed, blah. One of the most high-profile cases is the partial dissolution of a platinum statue in front of the United Monolith Corporation world headquarters."

Anna stops reading. "That explains a lot."

"I wonder if they'll ever try to take down the Monolith," Simon cannot help himself from wondering out loud.

"They seem more like the replacing-stone-with-other-things crowd around here."

"Not headstones?"

"Nadia took me to this really intricate necropolis this morning, painted on the walls of a couple apartment buildings. So, sort of?"

"Sounds like a happy place."

"'Happy place'? Seriously? Do you really feel nothing for our parents?"

"No, not really. Wait, I do feel curious, if that counts."

"You're like a sociopath or something."

"That's harsh and inaccurate. But I understand you're going through a difficult time, so I'll let it pass."

"Don't you have papers to grade?"

"I was grading them just fine thank you very much until you decided to show up and read Wikipedia articles out loud. Maybe you should go back to school."

"I never want to go back to that shithole."

"And yet, Monday will come and you'll be there."

"I'll get a GED instead."

"I don't think that'll be easier." Simon kicks himself for being sucked back into a conversation about his sister's issues. Saint Glinglin is a fun idea and would have made for a compelling heresy back in the day. He wants to visit the necropolis mural but not with Anna. It could even inspire a new themed party to replace Artichoke Day. The question of whether there are any other murals about burns on his tongue. He swallows it back and refocuses on the paper he is in the middle of grading.

Anna in turn resumes reading the results of her search, only now to herself. A comfortable silence descends, accentuated by the regular sound of pages turning and the more random tapping at the keyboard. Three papers later, Simon goes to the kitchen to pour himself another cup of coffee. He pours one for his sister while he is there and brings it to her. Into the afternoon, they hear the faint sound of cladding being replaced on a building a block over, a truck pass and similar noises.

He looks up occasionally, checking for nothing in particular. He tries to imagine his sister disintegrating into a sobbing, burbling mess. The image does not come. She has always been driven and frustrated in equal measure. The fish-jesus obsession is only the latest in a long line of passions she has borrowed. The problem always comes with transforming passions into projects that can be cut up into bite-sized chunks.

She has tried to trace a path from here to there, and he has tried to help. Narrowing her grand vision, cutting off the countless branches, has always ended in a sort of creative paralysis. Continuing with the tree analogy, it is also unhelpful the closer the defined path comes to the topmost branch, the more obvious the distance from the sun becomes. He decides the analogy does not work, as it implies success would be tantamount to an Icarus-like failure. She is far more the sort of person to jump off a roof and twist her ankle than to fly to the sun and fall to her death.

Anna's phone vibrates, breaking the spell of relaxed domesticity. A quick exchange of text messages follows. Then she closes the laptop.

"I'm going to meet Nadia," she says flatly.

"Not at school, I presume?"

"The day's over anyway."

"Would it be out of place to say 'have fun'?"

"Yes."

"Have fun!"

Anna grabs her bag and heads downstairs. Simon opens the laptop lid to see what she was searching. The most recent topics turn out to be around the Leeds music scene and art schools in the late seventies. The subject is unexpected but not exactly surprising or alarming. He quickly closes the lid and returns to the papers, unwilling to lose the momentum he has inadvertently built up.

10

Anna is delving into the history of the music scene Helen mentioned when her phone vibrates. A message from Nadia pops up asking to borrow the key to the museum. The request strikes Anna as odd since the only times Nadia has been to the museum were with her and, as far as she knows, the place is still open. She asks why in a variety of ways but Nadia evades the questions. Nadia finally asks if they can meet at a spot in the middle of the checkerboard.

Suddenly, Anna feels stuck in her brother's loop or box or whatever. He does not own the house but it still feels like his domain. The only idea she could hold onto last night to not break down was Theodore of Byzantium. This morning she searched for more—she does not even know what to call it; support? inspiration? distraction?—from the day calendar. It was his friendship with Tony that got her involved in the museum in the first place. She needed some sort of community service beyond Surget's influence, away from the assorted boxes of the school, and ended up trading one confined space for another. It is not Simon's fault. She feels grateful for what he has done. No, it is her failing.

She gets up and tells her brother she is going to meet Nadia. His final "have fun!" follows her into the street. Walking along the perfectly aligned roads, catching glimpses of the Monolith towering over the neighbourhood, the feeling of simply trading boxes grows stronger. From her perspective, it has always been this way. The houses that existed before are just so many stories Tony recounts. Yet she has never felt so constrained.

Nadia is sitting on the curb in front of an apartment building with a sign reading The Belle of Bâle next to a barren elm tree, tapping on her phone. Anna sits beside her and waits for the conversations with the absent to wind up.

"You left pretty abruptly at lunchtime," Nadia states.

"I'm not good company today. Didn't want to drag everyone down."

"I told you; if it was a problem to invite them, I wouldn't."

"It wasn't a problem. You can't spend all your time trying to cheer me up."

"You didn't even say anything before you left."

"You were a bit occupied with Martin, might as well have hung a sock on, I don't know, anything handy."

"We were keeping it PGish—not M at any rate."

"It was enough. Let's move on."

"Lettuce. Do you have the key?"

"Yes. Why?"

"It's best you don't know."

"But it's my key, it can be linked to me."

"I'm told City buildings have standard locks so maintenance and operations crews can access them whenever they need to. They aren't special high-security locks, the keys don't have unique tracking devices or anything. If a key happens to get copied, no one will know it's yours."

"But why would...someone wants to steal the shield? Who? Saint Glinglin disciples?"

"What does it matter?"

"What are you involved in? Is this why you don't have time to start a band?"

"Not something you should know about and maybe. I don't know. You'd probably want to rehearse on weekends; I'm usually off skiing or hiking."

"I want in."

"To what?"

"Whatever it is you're not telling me."

"For the sake of argument, let's say there is something. Let's say you're right all the way down the line: Saint Glinglin plans to steal the shield. What could you possibly do? What role do you picture yourself playing?"

"Dunno. Could help plan it. I know the building pretty well."

"That's actually a fair point—it's hard to keep track of the maze of rooms in that palace. You don't see yourself actually being part of the burglary?"

"I don't think I do all that great under pressure. Could be a look-out, I guess."

"Can you just give me your key?"

"Why not break in? Why should it seem like an inside job?"

"Maybe because Uni-lith doesn't own the building. As someone said earlier today, it matters who gets hurt."

"So it is Saint Glinglin." Anna pauses. "Why did you say 'Saint Glinglin plans to steal the shield,' like it's the saint himself who's going to do it?"

"It's not really the time to explain, is it?"

"I looked them up after I left. This would be just like them, or at least some splinter group. Are you part of the Saint Glinglin radical fringe? That would be brilliant! It would be this whole global feud that boils down to how your mom chose Uni-lith over her family. She's the villain of the first season but is turned back to the good side at the last minute when she realizes she is just a corporate puppet. She sacrifices herself to save you at the end of the final episode. Stay tuned for season two to find out if she survives. Everyone's checked the cast listing for season two, episode one. The actress playing your mom's there but maybe she's just in a flashback to give your character some extra pathos.

Now I'm starting to sound like you."

"You're not going to give me the key, are you?"

"On one condition. Let's pretend there really is going to be a burglary and you're part of it. We need to have burners with each other's number. If something goes wrong, we have to have a way to stay in contact."

"Fine. Theoretically."

Anna gives Nadia her key.

"I guess I shouldn't be surprised by your excitement," Nadia says. "You were pretty enthusiastic earlier about the idea of blowing up the Monolith. You say you need to cry but maybe punching something would do you one better. Thanks for the key."

Nadia walks off. Anna is left, not sure what to do or where to go. The story of her life. The notebook with the sketchy beginning of The Ear Stone Chronicles is in her bag. It is the only thing she feels is her own, yet she has nothing to show for it. She is too scared to pull it out, convinced as she is she will not be able to write anything, or at least anything that will not weigh on her later. The fear turns her away from the idea of going to a café on the main street or to the southern edge of the neighbourhood. The last thing she wants is to feel even more like a failure. But then going back to the house, or anywhere else, seems even worse.

A couple minutes later, Nadia returns. "Come on," she says. Anna follows without a word. The two head east toward downtown, past the main street and through the eclectic foothills. As they pass the main street, Nadia opens up.

"I posted the video I took of the shield this morning. It turned out to be the most popular thing I have ever posted. Ever. The comments quickly went off the rails. There is a lot of envy, greed, lust and all the rest in the world. For a fleeting moment, it all seemed directed at this one object. I was more amazed at the reaction than at the shield itself, which is saying something."

They contemplate the nature of humanity as laid bare by the pseudo-anonymity of the internet as they go by short, balcony-studded towers interspersed with row houses and bungalows. Office blocks are added to the mix and bungalows become rarer as the blocks progress. When they reach the edge of the business district, Nadia goes into a shoe repair and key cutting hole in the wall. Anna waits outside. She scans the street, taking in the variety of suits, business casual, casual and slept in. Adam crosses her mind; it was jarring to see a security guard in his place this morning. Despite last night's drama, she had put some empty bottles in her bag to give to him. Their occasional clanking reminds her intermittently she still has them.

She has yet to really think through the impact of the museum's transformation on the other misfits who have been using it as a sort of refuge. The only other place in the neighbourhood with benches and no anti-homeless controls is the promenade overlooking the drop-off. Adam might have even been there last night. It turns out trying to not completely fall apart makes one pretty oblivious to the world. She promises herself to make more of an effort to get the bottles to him.

Pulling out her phone, she also texts Simon, suggesting he invites Tony over that evening. She has no idea how deep the whole Saint Anthony hermit thing goes. Tony could have a wife, kids and a goldfish for all she knows. From the little she recalls about Saint Anthony from the repartee between her brother and Tony, the hermit was never truly alone. He had his faith, God and the communal pig. He only struggled with being abandoned when the temptations invaded.

She never pictured Tony as alone even when he was literally by himself, taking down or putting up an exhibit or waiting for one of the rare visitors to pass through the red door. A major temptation camping out in the middle of the space has undoubtedly changed the dynamic however. It makes her uncomfortable to rely once more on Simon's view of the world, even if it is such a convenient way to express how Tony might be feeling. The important thing is to be supportive; nobody cares if he really fits the saintly mold.

Nadia exits the shop and hands Anna her key and a cheap-looking flip phone.

"It isn't happening tonight, is it?" Anna asks.

Nadia shrugs and starts walking back to the checkerboard. Anna follows.

"It can't happen tonight. Nobody knew the shield was going to be there until it showed up last night. There wouldn't be enough time to plan it. Unless they have an inside man, I guess."

"Only it's a woman and it turns out to be my mom. According to the TV show, anyway."

"I do think your mom is evil genius material."

"You're just saying that because she's a scientist."

"Pretty much. But also the whole soulless multinational corporation thing. It's how you describe her, by the way."

"You need to come up with something more original."

"That's never going to happen."

"You're selling yourself short. There's an evil genius in all of us just waiting to come out."

"The title of your new self-help book?"

"My contribution to The Ear Stone Chronicles. My mom can be a model for one of the characters. You have my permission." Nadia pulls out her phone and looks at it briefly. "I'm going to have to leave you behind once we get to the main street."

"For good?"

"For good. You'll have to fend for yourself like a big girl."

They walk for a while longer.

"What a strange day," Anna comments as they approach the street. "Usually, your nose would be glued to your phone. Martin will be worried. Don't they always say you're supposed to act normally under these circumstances?"

"It's easy for you to say. I always just say whatever comes to mind and now I have to question every word. It's too much. No matter what I do, it comes out all weird. Ech!"

"Good luck tonight."

"I don't know what you're talking about." Nadia walks off, leaving Anna for a second time that afternoon. Nadia makes it as far as the end of the block before coming back.

"That was quick," Anna says.

"Kevin wanted me to give this to you," Nadia says, handing Anna an odd-shaped object wrapped in brown paper. "He wanted to give it to you himself but you slunk away at lunch."

Not bothering to open the package, Anna stashes it in her bag. Nadia immediately turns away, this time definitively disappearing from sight.

Anna considers wandering around to try to find Adam but figures it will be better if she stays still and waits for him to come by. While the day is sunnier and warmer than yesterday, it is still too cool for her to be comfortable stuck in one place outside for very long. So, she sucks in her breath and finds a spot in a café overlooking the street.

Once installed, a cup of coffee on the table in front of her, she steels herself once more and pulls out her notebook. It surprises her the page topped by The Ear Stone Chronicles looks exactly the same as it did when she was sitting on a blanket in the museum, propped up by a pile of pillows, in the company of a horde of artichokes and not at all aware her parents might be dead. The fact that nothing else changed does not affect her in any way, other than perhaps confirming her suspicion that the world is a cold and indifferent place.

This page should be different however. It is intimately linked to her. At the most basic level, like the statoliths in creatures that never evolved hearing, it should still at the very least be sensitive to changes in gravity and momentum. It should resonate with her loss of balance. There should no longer be an obvious top from where to start nor a direction from any point. Even if the server dropped off an alien pen at that very moment, gifting her with unlimited imagination, there should be no way to anchor that creativity to the paper.

If she was to press her ear to the page, she should come away with an amorphous ringing. It should be as if an explosion just went off, leaving resounding deafness in its wake. Bystanders have rushed in to help, are repeating "Are you okay?" endlessly. None of the words penetrate the auditory haze.

The alien pen should fare no better, be filled with white ink. It can only add weight to the white noise without ever managing to differentiate itself. Ideas surpassing those imagined by Shakespeare's muse spill out onto the paper only to be lost.

Instead, it is an ordinary page, dumb to what she feels. It lays there in front of her, passively awaiting some sort of expression, powerful vibrations muted by the mediation of language. The Ear Stone Chronicles are stories told through the fundamental pull of the earth and other celestial bodies on all life. They are stories prior even to the rhythmic oscillations of music. Anna cannot decide how far into pretentiousness she has gone with the description but is pretty sure the answer is very far. She fights paralysis, uncaps her ordinary pen and adds some aimless blue ink to the sheet.

Documentary or infomercial: Goats in Space. An interview with the chief of an asteroid mining crew digging into a planetoid off Jupiter for the intragalactic corporation Consolidated Aerolithics. He describes the permanent sensation of falling when one is in orbit. Humans, lemmings and a whole variety of other creatures get used to the feeling. Goats do not. They panic at random times and, even dehorned, are able to damage the platform and hurt the crew.

Artificial gravity is out of the question, as it is expensive, finicky and a pain to calibrate. The company would be forced to add another crew member just to make sure it worked properly for the duration of the assignment. The crew can live without goats, though the beasts are more compact than cows and sheep and fresh milk ensures calcium intake is up and does wonders for morale. He is referring of course to the morale of the human crew—goat morale has yet to be measured.

Ear Stones were the solution we were looking for. It is a minor surgical procedure that embeds a small magnet in the goat's inner ear. The magnet pulls toward the floor of the platform, giving her an impression of up and down in line with her other senses. It is not strong and the sensation of falling persists but it suffices for keeping her calm.

A car alarm goes off. Anna looks up to see dusk has descended. The street is gridlocked; evening rush hour is at its height. The sun is replaced by a thousand lights but they cannot compete. The café is filling up with white-collar workers, stopping in for a quick drink with colleagues and friends before heading home to family or loneliness. She realizes how terrible a job she has been doing in looking for Adam, though is momentarily content to have written something.

The goat idea is silly and far too entangled with her parents. It is however something; maybe even something that beats both violence and sadness. She only wishes she could trust it but knows from experience such a sentiment is unreliable, fleeting. She needs the alien pen; a solid object she can pull out and use. Gazing at the cars stuttering by, her opinion shifts. Space goats are not silly, they are stupid. She finally manages to string a couple sentences together in a coherent way and she ends up with garbage. "Garbage" is exactly the word. She tears the page out of the notebook, crumples it into a compact ball and stuffs it into her nearly empty cup. The paper slowly absorbs the coffee, becoming a splotchy brown.

Helen tells her—no, it was just a suggestion—to join a band and the first thing she does is try to get involved in some unholy mix of cultishness, terrorism and thievery. She wonders what is wrong with her. The answer comes immediately: everything. Everything is broken. She should not be so dramatic; everything is twisted. And all she gets out of the bargain are space goats.

Cars start to flow more smoothly, drawing her eyes and thoughts along. The vast majority of drivers are simply passing through from their offices downtown to their homes in the suburbs. Some can probably see the checkerboard and the Monolith from the skyscrapers where they work, a perfectly regular anomaly in the urban fabric. A curiosity, nothing more. By the time they reach this point in their commute, they are already absorbed by the thousand little pathologies of the neighbourhoods at the edge of town.

The cars' lights suddenly disappear behind a mass of darkness. Anna blinks several times and refocuses. Her brain slowly transfers power from self-flagellation to image recognition. She starts to make out Adam. Then she realizes it really is Adam, the person she has supposedly been looking for. She taps on the window until he turns to look and then motions for him to join her. He shakes his head, so she signals him to stay where he is. Not waiting for a response, she tosses her notebook in her bag and goes to settle up, leaving the space goats behind.

The cold air hits her on the way out. She pulls her jacket tighter and curses Adam's obstinacy in not joining her inside. Standing beside him and his ever-present shopping cart, she sets her bag on the ground, shifts Kevin's package to the side and grabs the six-pack.

"Adam." She gives the empty bottles to him.

"Anna," he mumbles, taking the bottles and putting them in the garbage bag laying on the miscellanea in his cart. He then pushes the bag to the side and digs into his collection of objects. He comes up with a Buddy Christ figure melded with a fish tail, which he gives to Anna.

"Wow!" Anna exclaims. "It's like Buddy Christ of the mermaids— Buddy Merchrist. If I remembered any of the songs from The Little Mermaid, I'd be singing right now. Thanks, Adam!"

Adam shrugs. "Wouldn't it be 'mermen'?"

"Yeah, probably. Hard to check between the legs though, with the tail and everything."

"I wanted to give it to you this morning."

"You went to the museum?"

He nods.

"Things sure have changed."

"The guard told me to move on. I didn't want any trouble."

"Uni-lith taking over everything really sucks but I guess that's what they do. Didn't think they'd ever be interested in the museum though. Where do you go now?"

He shrugs.

"We can't just stand here. Want to go to the promenade?"

He shrugs undecidedly but finally nods. They start walking south. Anna's phone vibrates. Simon says Tony has accepted the invitation and will arrive in a couple hours. While she is looking at her phone, Adam mumbles under his breath, "Don't recognize that guy."

A block later, she abruptly stops and asks, "What guy?"

He turns and nods toward a panhandler sitting on the sidewalk behind them. She takes in the scene; cars now moving fluidly, after-work drinkers filtering out onto the sidewalk. The museum is perhaps not directly across the street but close enough.

"Do you know all the panhandlers on the street?" she asks.

He shrugs. "Some. Not the most profitable street. There aren't that many."

She looks again. The thought crosses her mind that it could be some Saint Glinglin follower casing the joint. Sitting on the sidewalk, the view would be blocked by the cars though. It would make more sense to find a spot in a café, like she did. Deciding to play lookout even if nothing was happening tonight, she fishes in her bag for the burner and texts Nadia, "suspicious beggar across the street. A doesn't recognize him." Adam waits patiently and quietly. The message sent, they continue on their way.

"Are your parents still alive?" she asks.

He shakes his head.

"I just learned mine are gone. Yesterday."

"I'm sorry."

"How did you cope?"

"I didn't."

"That's how I feel. Just lost. Do you have family around?"

"A brother." Adam stops and sifts through his collection of objects. He pulls out a small plastic bag a moment later, from which he takes an envelope, which is opened in turn to reveal a Christmas card. Folded into the card is a picture of a young boy and girl on Santa's lap. He hands the photo to Anna. "His kids," he explains.

"They're cute. Do you see them often?"

He shakes his head, takes the picture back and rewraps it with care.

"That sucks."

"It's better for them."

"Still. And your brother?"

"No."

"My brother is my only family. Sometimes I think we're too close, like I'm constantly running into his ideas in my head. He's brilliant, you know. The things he thinks up are so much better than anything I can come up with. I kind of hate it."

"Was fish-jesus his idea?"

"I bet you think it's strange. I mean, it is strange. That's the point, really. To have this symbol so off-the-wall that it can't help but free the imagination. Didn't come from my brother, not his style. His stuff seems crazy too, but it's a grounded sort of crazy. Like some time, thousands of years ago, there actually was a group of people who truly believed it. Or there was some super-important novel that was tripped up over the issue. Everything my space goats lack."

Anna pulls one of the day calendar pages out of her pocket. "Ophites," she reads, "were a sect from second century Egypt that worshiped the serpent." She looks up. "I'm guessing it's the whole temptation thing from the Garden of Eden."

"Just as Moses lifted up the snake in the wilderness, so the Son of Man must be lifted up."

"That sounds like a quote. Is that a quote?"

Adam nods.

"See, I was going to just go with the obvious explanation that some people were tempted by temptation, which seems inevitable if you think about it. But now you're telling me there's a whole other angle here, which doesn't surprise me at all. That's the sort of thing my brother comes up with; odd and amusing even if you don't know anything about anything, like me, but with a lot of meat if you want to dig into it. He whipped up a whole day calendar out of these heresies. I keep it in my locker at school.

"Fish-jesus didn't come from me either; I got it from a musician I admire. Ever been in a band?"

"I like the pianos someone put out last summer. I hope they do it again this year."

"Do you play?"

"No. But it's nice."

"I think so too."

They arrive at the promenade. Adam goes to the same bench he sat on yesterday, Anna following along. The mix of people is similar. Anna looks around before sitting, wondering if there is anyone who was here last night. She was so absorbed trying to dig up family memories and replaying the flower being reduced to powder. The only things that registered were the darkness right in front of her and the railing keeping people from falling into it.

She notices most benches are occupied by two people, though it is often unclear whether they know each other or not. "I suppose the question really is: do you want to see more of your family? Is the relationship with them what you chose or was it them?"

He stares into the darkness and takes his time responding. "Choice," he ends up repeating, shaking his head. "What choice?"

"Dunno." The choice seems obvious to her. Her parents' decision could not have been clearer. They did not choose to die but they sure did decide to spend an awful lot of time in a well-known zone of armed conflict, if not outright war. But if Adam is able to quote from what she assumes is the Bible, maybe he thinks there is a divine plan. She recalls vaguely hearing that one of the principles of Alcoholics Anonymous and the like was accepting one's helplessness and seeking guidance from a higher power. What are the chances he has never had issues with booze, pills or whatever else?

The thought pops into her head that her joking about heresies could be deeply offensive. He could simply be too beaten down by life to say anything. She could be not so different from the Uni-lith security guard in his eyes—he doesn't want trouble. She is at a loss to continue the conversation.

"All love is conditional," Adam says after a time.

"Oh?" Anna replies, now really confused. Is the love of Christ not supposed to be unconditional? Merchrist would be pickier, she decides to herself. It slowly dawns on her that Adam really followed through; she has her wonderfully ridiculous totem. Regardless of everything else going on in the world, she has been blessed with a symbol. It changes absolutely nothing, yet it still means so much.

He does not expand on his declaration.

"Well, if that's so, you've certainly bought my devotion with Buddy Merchrist." Ideas start bubbling up and she does not hold them in. "Like Jesus, only he really slept with the fishes. Amazes the crowd by walking on land. Changes wine into water, so, you know, he can breathe."

"That's not very funny."

"But it's distracting, which is even better. Who needs to cry or punch things when bad jokes will do the trick?"

The two look out into the darkness in silence. Nothingness would be good too, Anna thinks, but it's just an illusion. Some distance behind them, they hear the rapid steps of someone running and jumping over obstacles. Moments later, a figure in dark clothing clears an empty bench and then vaults over the railing. The sound of sliding follows, chaotic, down the steep, uneven slope, before stopping abruptly.

Witnesses, unsure as to what they just saw, belatedly react. Several people go to the railing and peer into the abyss. A couple of them pull out phones to use as flashlights but the light is too weak to illuminate the quickly receding ground. Someone calls into the darkness, "Are you okay?" Another echoes the call.

A discussion ensues on whether to call an ambulance or the police. Someone notices a squad car is slowly moving down the street and flags it down. The crowd is soon joined by a police officer and a Uni-lith security guard, whose flashlights reveal a grassy slope lost about ten metres down in a thick wood. No traces of the darkly clad figure are visible. Minutes later, what remains of the promenade's peaceful ambiance is drowned out by the sound of a helicopter.

The crowd at the railing peaks and then starts to dissipate. The helicopter circles wider before heading north. The officer and guard return to their car and slowly drive off. The pitch of conversations is higher, more excited. Idle speculation builds, people start checking their phones for news to feed into it.

Throughout the spectacle, Anna and Adam stay on their bench.

"I guess I was expecting a spotlight from the helicopter," she says.

"Thermal imaging."

"Oh. Makes sense."

"There's camps down there."

"Homeless camps? On the slope?"

"Transient camps, in the woods."

"So finding one person would be pretty hard."

"Unless they're running or sliding."

"Right. Our moment of excitement for the day."

"I hope they didn't get hurt."

"Why? What's the point? Anyone who jumps over the railing is practically begging to be hurt. They probably did all sorts of stuff before this just as risky. Sure, okay, mitigating circumstances and all the rest. You can't tell me they didn't choose."

"I still hope they didn't get hurt."

"You should be hoping they die a quick death and save your good thoughts for all of us on this side of the barrier. You should be hoping they don't become a burden on the rest of us because of their foolishness. You should be hoping they don't hurt anyone else."

She pauses, giving him a chance to agree or at least argue. He does neither. Her phone vibrates. Simon is letting her know Tony has arrived and reminds her it was her idea to invite him.

"Look, you shouldn't wish anyone's death," she nuances. "I didn't mean that at all. You just can't care about people like that. They won't care and you'll feel like shit."

She pauses again.

"I have to go. Thanks for listening. Thanks for Merchrist, it really does mean a lot."

"Sorry about your parents," he finally speaks.

"Yeah, well...thanks."

She walks back into the checkerboard. From a distance, she can see an area of the main street cordoned off. The scene does not arouse her curiosity, just the desire to avoid more, and probably unnecessary, drama. Before walking through her door, she makes an effort to put herself in the mindset to laugh at the hermit jokes, if not to accept her brother's vision of the world more generally.

11

"Why are we still talking about it?" Saint Glinglin asks all the other Saint Glinglins in the room in an exasperated tone.

Nadia, as Saint Glinglin, and several others nod their heads and say, "Hear, hear!" Others grumble semi-intelligibly about the true meaning of Glinglin.

A dissenting Glinglin speaks up: "The notion is to wipe out the symbol of patriarchy. It is the statue in the public square, the cross or minaret. It's public, visible, high-profile. It's everything the shield is not."

An assenting Glinglin counters: "It's a sculptural symbol of United Monolith, the largest of our corporate masters and it's in a public museum. How does that not fit the definition?"

"All technicalities. Nobody ever visits the museum; it's practically a tomb for odds and ends not a single soul cares about. United Monolith may have used the shield as part of their corporate identity for a brief instant twenty years ago but not since then. If you went outside today with a picture of it and asked everyone who passed what it meant, no one would be able to tell you. The only thing anyone sees today is an enormous mass of gold."

A second assenting Glinglin pipes up: "The gold is a symbol in itself, of the unchecked accumulation of wealth and power of our overlords. It's even worse it's thrown into a so-called tomb. The value of that mass of gold could end homelessness in the city forever. But United Monolith sees it as a trinket, a knickknack."

A random Glinglin adds, "A bauble."

The first dissenting Glinglin replies, "It is a trinket compared to United Monolith's power. I'm all for redistribution—and that's a whole lot of gold—but don't dress it up as fulfilling the vision of Saint Glinglin. Grab it and give it to the poor, don't dissolve it as if that has any impact, symbolic or real, on United Monolith. We'd be better off blowing up the Monolith."

A second dissenter adds: "We're so focused on the shield we've lost sight of Saint Glinglin's teachings. The son destroyed the machine that kept the rain at bay. The subsequent deluge was what dissolved the monolith but it also fundamentally changed the society. Dissolving the shield has drowned out any discussion about breaking the machine. Yet it's only through breaking the machine that we'll change anything. It's like we've swapped consequence for cause."

The exasperated Saint Glinglin, the informal chair of the meeting, tries to ground the discussion. "You are all blowing this out of proportion. Dissolving the shield is a low-risk opportunity that dropped in our lap. Our fellow Saint Glinglins around the world have developed a relatively easy process for it—though obviously the chemicals are still really dangerous. We've been looking for an opportunity, somewhere between murals and blowing up the Monolith, to act. Here it is, so let's just do it. It doesn't stop us from breaking the machine later. In fact, this is the sort of experience we need to succeed at more high-profile actions later on. View it as a live trial run, not a deep philosophical quandary."

A round of vocal "hear, hear!" follows. Nadia sort of figured the meeting would be full of endless discussion and hand-wringing. She had hoped for an experience similar to the boulderless bouldering; silent and efficient. The long-winded theologizing was always present though, just woven into the murals.

The dozen Saint Glinglins are gathered in an empty basement apartment. The walls are a freshly painted white, the carpeting and flooring spotless and all the appliances absent. A table, chairs and lamps are the only furniture. Everyone around the table wears dark, unassuming street clothes. Everything but the discussion points to a quick, final meeting after the equipment is loaded up but before taking action.

The second dissenter says, "I don't know how we can do this in the name of Saint Glinglin. It will be giving people the wrong idea."

The first dissenter, wavering, argues, "If it's really a lead up to something more important, I guess that works. It would be nice to get some practice in before blowing up the Monolith."

A random Glinglin remarks, "We're never going to blow up the Monolith."

The exasperated Glinglin tempers, "Let's not say what we will or won't do in the future. For today, the goal is the shield. After that's done, we can decide how best to move forward. Agreed?"

The second dissenter replies, "So long as we don't claim it as Saint Glinglin."

The first assenter says, "If we can dissolve the whole thing, if that much gold goes down the drain, we're claiming it."

A random Glinglin: "Will it ruin the pipes?"

"I'm speaking metaphorically."

"Oh."

The second dissenter: "It's fundamentally wrong-headed. Even if it's a spectacular success, it's not Saint Glinglin."

Exasperated Glinglin: "Tabling the credit idea. Dissolving the shield, yay or nay?"

After an elbow to the second dissenter's ribs, all say "yay."

"Everyone knows their role?"

Nadia, as Saint Glinglin, is the sole person to say "no."

"Keep close to me, open the door, carry what I hand you."

"Got it."

"And, everyone, go to the washroom before we leave."

A couple Glinglins do exactly that. Then the group piles into three grey Honda Accords from a variety of years parked at the back of the building. The dissent, exasperation and other divisions melt away, leaving a simple multiplication of Saint Glinglin. The cars take different routes through the checkerboard; one relatively direct, the other two meandering.

The first car enters the relaxed flow of traffic on the main street.

The road is starting to fill with drivers circling between drags with bars and clubs, replacing those in a hurry to get home. Leaving the main flow of traffic, the car turns left during the brief moment offered by the changing traffic lights. It immediately turns right down the alley behind the row of well-lit shops and restaurants and pulls into the gravel parking lot at the back of the museum.

All the Glinglins exit the vehicle. Two cause a racket, ostensibly trying to find a way through the fence. The other two hurry down the alley and make a noisy scene up the block. The second Accord stops on a side street with a clear view of the front of the museum. The United Monolith guard leaves his post, first trying to find a direct way around the museum and then entering the building. A couple minutes after that, he exits and walks around the block to get to the alley. Once he has turned the corner, the Accord crosses the flow of traffic and stops in front. The last car joins the second moments later.

Trunks are popped. One Glinglin opens the red door; the seven others quickly and efficiently carry materials into the museum. The narrow windows are papered over and two floodlights set up. They then start to assemble a portable vat. By the time the guard returns to his post, the only sign of their presence is the two cars.

Nadia, idle while the others work, finds her individuality creeping back. She is impressed by how well the team works together. They may have their differences but they know when to shut up and get shit done. In retrospect, the bitching session before the job looks like just another part of their process; a programmed letting off of steam so they are not tempted to theologize at an inopportune moment.

This is the first time she has been in the room without the curtains. The bare white walls, combined with the cold lights and concrete floor, give the space the feeling of a miniature warehouse. It is unclear if the pile of painting supplies in one corner is being stored or is there to be used. Sounds are intensified as they bounce off the hard surfaces. Despite Saint Glinglin's efforts to work quietly, the room is brimming with noise. The feeling is completely alien to the sleepy mornings spent in the mauve corner with Anna, brainstorming ideas for The Ear Stone Chronicles.

They were so bad at coming up with anything. Just staying awake was a struggle for her but that did not explain their block. They are able to come up with all sorts of random and amusing ideas all day long. There was something about taking it seriously and recording everything they came up with that took away their spontaneity. All at once, they did not trust themselves.

In that way, Saint Glinglin is inspiring. It is not just his purposefulness and, when it comes down to it, lack of hesitation in dissolving the shield. Every mural she has seen is masterfully done. He has clear ideas and is able to transform them into something concrete and, as far as she is concerned, amazing. Somehow, all of that is compatible with continuing to question what it even means to be Saint Glinglin. While it is good Anna is not here, she could probably use some of his insight.

Thinking about Anna, Nadia pulls the burner phone out of her pocket. She is surprised to see a text: "suspicious beggar across street. A doesn't recognize him." It is not immediately obvious to her who "A" is, let alone the importance of an odd panhandler. As Saint Glinglin finishes putting the vat together and seals it, she mulls the message over. Cans of yellow-orange liquid are brought next to the shield and everyone puts on gas masks. Nadia moves a can and dons her mask a beat after everyone else.

The first fragment that fits into place is that Anna is talking about Adam. The next, that the transient might be a phony. A third of the Glinglins are outside, so she imagines the panhandler could be one of them. That is not part of the plan as she understands it. On the other hand, she is not privy to very much. She holds the question in, knowing speaking is contrary to the efficient unfolding of the project.

The third fragment starts a cascade. The shield is Uni-lith property, protected by Uni-lith security. From her experience visiting her mom at work when she was younger, one guard does seem light. She had not questioned it, given the ugliness of the shield and the low-key nature of the museum, but it would make sense to have more agents around. Disguises are not really Uni-lith's thing, unless it is a trap. Saint Glinglin had damaged company property before, so this could be a way to draw them out. It is actually pretty obvious, now she thinks it through.

"It's a trap!" she says excitedly, her voice muffled by the mask. She repeats it louder, this time aiming for alarm rather than excitement. All eyes turn to her and the noise of pouring the first can into the vat tails off. At that moment, she is the other; the stranger in the room being judged by Saint Glinglin. She finds herself completely indifferent to what the team thinks and busies herself with coming up with her own escape plan.

The sound of sirens approaching ends the silent interrogation. The floodlights are turned off and the Glinglins, as one, move toward the back door. Nadia, breaking away, scales the vat and then the statue. Saint Glinglin jumps out the back, passes through a newly cut hole in the fence and climbs into the waiting cars, one of the Accords having been driven around while he was inside. Nadia climbs one of the piano straps and breaks a pane of the skylight. The glass shatters noisily on the floor.

The red door bursts open as the glass hits and a mix of police officers and United Monolith guards pours in. They slow as the acid fumes reach them but, with multiple openings allowing the vapours to quickly dissipate, continue on. Their eyes are drawn to where the glass just broke and then to the wide-open door at the back. The sound of cars starting and maneuvering leads most to run directly to the back. The few more cautious agents sweep the room with their flashlights, including up to the skylight. By that time, Nadia is no longer visible and they do not see a practical way to climb up to the roof.

Nadia quickly decides, with only one building to the north of the museum, south is the only direction that makes sense. The distance to the building to the south is easily four metres. She runs a loop around the museum roof to build up momentum before reaching the jumping-off point, relying on the ornate cornice to keep her hidden from the ground until she is in the air. More sirens approach, covering the sound of her leap. She lands off balance, collapses into a roll and pushes herself awkwardly to the side as she sees how close she is coming to a brightly-lit skylight.

Adrenaline gives her the force to hop back up and keep going. The next four roofs are flush and the fifth only a metre and a half away. The heights vary but, with the help of some conveniently located mechanical equipment, she is able to scramble across them without much trouble. She stops dead at a parking lot before the last building on the block, drops to her stomach and crawls to the edge. A roadblock is set in the alley, lights flashing, sirens silenced. One of the Accords is stopped and some of the newly disaggregated Glinglins are being arrested. The main street at the end of the block is being cordoned off. She realizes she is about to be cornered.

The parking lot is about half full. She chooses a spot next to a van and drops off the roof as quietly as she can. Crawling under the vehicle, she gets her bearings. Boots cross back and forth between the street and the alley right in front of her. Voices fade in and out, talking about the multiple cars, one of which managed to get past before they were able to block the roads. They bring up Tony Abbott but she does not catch what exactly they are saying about him.

When the boots are as far away as possible, she crawls out from under the van and makes her way, squatted down, across the lot. It extends behind the last building, giving her a route to the cross street. When no one is looking, she pops up and walks over to a police car. She gets an officer's attention and asks him with wide-eyed innocence what is going on. He gives her vague answers about a robbery and asks what she is doing out. She replies she was supposed to meet a friend at a café on the block but now she does not know what to do. He suggests she go home. If her friend is in the café she—Nadia corrects him with a "he"—should stay there and, if not, he should go home too. She thanks him and walks away.

A Uni-lith guard looks at her suspiciously but does not intervene. She crosses the street and then, without stopping, glances back. The guard and the officer are looking at her, talking and gesturing. If they call her back or start following her, she figures she has two options. She can either play the daughter of the head of the Monolith card or she can run. The guard crosses the street through traffic, calling "miss" and waving at her. There is no way in hell she is going to lean on her mom, so she breaks into a run. She zigzags east and south through the foothills. She is less familiar with it than the checkerboard but familiar enough to lose her pursuers.

She hears a helicopter. Though it sounds a fair distance away, she aims to limit as much as possible the risk of being spotted. She picks up the pace and veers south. Because of the terrain, the drop off is not regularly policed. The forces of order occasionally make a point of sweeping it, though only to dismantle homeless camps before they become too established. The couple times she has participated in ravine spring clean-up with her dad, that has always been part of the orientation. They are to pick up the litter people throw over the edge but not approach any camps. She made a snide comment one time about the camps being full of people society threw away, which did not go over well.

She abruptly emerges from among the varied buildings, darkness filling her vision. Angling for an unoccupied bench, she jumps over it and then clears the railing. She lands in a controlled slide down the grassy slope. Everything is going well until she reaches the woods, where the ground is still wet from the snow the day before. Her feet suddenly slip out from under her and she lands hard on her back. The wind is knocked out of her and the slide continues.

Grabbing at whatever she can to slow herself down, branches and grass break off and pull out in her hands. She finally grips the trunk of a small tree with one hand. Her shoulder feels like it is being pulled out of its socket as her body's forward momentum is absorbed. Continuing to fight for breath, the pain passes in silence.

She pivots around the trunk and finally comes to a stop when her head smacks against a rock.

The boarding school's chapel is empty at this time of night. Nadia moves slowly, numbly through the space, crossing between the rows of pews. She expects the wood would be etched by the endless parade of boys who passed their formative years here, bored to death of the daily services given in an odd mix of Latin and Slovenian. Instead, it is just worn, tired. The feeling seeps into her and she slumps down in the middle of a bench.

At the front, framing the altar and cross, are shelves upon shelves of statues of saints. She has the feeling they are examining her, judging her deeds and words. It is suddenly obvious this is a conciliabule. At first blush, it seems they are deciding whether she is a heretic. She catches snippets of the conversation. They have come to a consensus that she is indeed a heretic, only they are not sure if she is significant enough to include in the calendar. The argument is between those who believe it is of no importance—they are a day short, so they need someone—and those who think it would dilute the message.

They decide to call on an expert. A door off to the side opens and her mother walks in. Of course, Nadia thinks to herself. She refuses to stay to hear her mom's take on her life, so struggles to her feet and drags them to the large door at the back. It is locked. She tries to force it but has no strength in her arms. A throbbing pain in her left shoulder comes to the fore, adding to the fatigue rather than distracting from it.

Giving up and turning to the room, she sees the cross has been replaced by the shield. She tries to run to another door, making it two steps before her chest tightens up, depriving her of oxygen. She drags herself to a pew and collapses once more, only this time laying on it. She does not understand what is happening, why her body is failing her. In the background, her mom is explaining how her precious daughter has been corrupted by Hellenistic heresies. Nadia closes her eyes and does her best to both ignore the voice and breathe normally.

The Hellenistic heresies, used to denigrate the sublime nature of the golden shield, are only the latest in a series of scandal-
ous ideas espoused. Her mom goes through the heresies she and
Anna joked about every morning in meticulous detail, starting with
the Adamites. Nadia's mind makes a vague connection between
Adamites and Adam, Adam and A, the warning and the trap. The
museum and the chapel meld together as one room whose sole purpose is to hold the gilded megalith.

The seemingly endless list of faults her mother intones takes on
a shade of needless rationalization. Her crime is against the stone;
the object at the centre of the room, the family, the society. Without
it, modern life falls apart. Even Saint Glinglin knows this. After the
son breaks the machine, dissolving the symbol of his father, he is
fated to sacrifice himself so the machine may function once more.

Nadia does not notice right away the shift in the discussion
from faults to punishment. When she does, she opens her eyes and
struggles up until she is sitting with a view of the shelves of saints
and her mother. The saints look especially wooden, her mom cold
and polished. She shivers, feeling as if her mom's presence is slowly
chilling the room.

Sanctions are tossed out, followed by protracted debates. She
is familiar with the ideas, though it takes her a while to place them.
It slowly occurs to her they are linked to the faults; they, at least
most of them, are punishments suffered by the heretics. There is no
reason to invent new tortures when they have so many ready-made
forms of cruelty to choose from. Her mom does not participate; instead she waits patiently for the discussion to run its course, indeci-
sion to set in and one of the saints to ask her to find a way out of the
impasse. Nadia is sure her mother has already decided her fate and
that the decision will ultimately be accepted by everyone.

The predictable stalemate sets in. The saints turn to Sara, who
instructs those not present—it is not really clear who—to bring in
the vat. The door at the back opens and a vat resembling the one
Saint Glinglin set up in the museum is brought in by generic Uni-

lith workers in white lab coats, company IDs displayed but perpetually out of focus. Nadia watches as the basin is carried by and the door snaps shut. When she turns back to the front, her mother is busy at a table with an elaborate chemistry set, mixing fuming, colourful chemicals.

She had vaguely anticipated more discussion, more theories and disagreements on how to inflict pain. Instead, the shelves of wooden saints look on approvingly, even eagerly. She hears a sound above her and looks up to see a pulley and harness being attached to one of the hanging straps. A moment ago, there were no straps, no chemicals, nothing but symbols, statues and words. The most distressing aspect was the chill emanating from her mother as she led the proceedings against the stranger who was her daughter.

Nadia's mind is stuck on the fact that there really is a vat and cans of yellow-orange acid. There really are straps and a golden shield. None of it can be dismissed as figments of her imagination, no matter how many pieces of the scene are out of place. And her body, every part of it though some parts more than others, hurts. Sitting upright somehow makes her hair hurt, which she is somewhat thankful for. It counterbalances the feeling her left arm is about to fall off and her lungs are incapable of expanding. If her mom's plan is to lower her into a vat of acid, there is no reason to think she will not suffer every excruciating second of her flesh disintegrating. She will probably scream in agony like the Nazis who open the Arc of the Covenant, if her lungs will let her.

The fumes start to obscure the table. Her mother, a beaker in hand, turns toward her for a second, face obscured by a gas mask. Nadia starts to panic. She knows that mask, it is the one Saint Glinglin uses; it is her mask. She wheezes in pain, trying to force her hands to feel if she still has a mask on. She knows her face is uncovered but what does she really know? Where did she leave her mask? The fumes spread, slowly filling the room.

"Mom. Please. Stop," she whispers as tears stream down her face. Her mother pays no attention. "Please. I'm begging you..." She has no more words, nothing to appeal to, either her mother is a monster or she is. A sharp, pungent smell suddenly hits her and the room disappears.

12

Sara is in her office, making the final touches to a posting for an intermediate physicist, when her phone rings. The call display reads Driss Rehg. She picks up the handset.

"Hi, it's Gavin calling from Driss Rehg's office."

"What can I do for you, Gavin?"

"Driss wanted me to let you know the announcement concerning the acquisition of Consolidated Aerolithics has been moved up."

"Okay. I didn't know a date had been set in the first place."

"Oh, that's true. Well, a date and time have now been chosen."

"And they would be..."

"Today, in an hour."

"That's fast. There hasn't been time to make any progress on the museum situation. Has Driss changed his mind regarding warming up local sentiment."

"I don't know anything about that."

"Do you know anything about why it's happening today?"

"This didn't come from me but there are apparently some rumours floating around about the demise of the president and CEO of Consolidated Aerolithics."

"I've heard those rumours."

"The plan is to get through the press conference before the only question is 'What happened to the Perennas?'"

"Any truth to the rumours?"

"I don't think so but not having an answer might make things worse."

"Yes, it might. What is my role in all this?"

"Driss only asked me to keep you informed."

"And you know nothing about the museum."

"No."

"Thank you for letting me know."

"It's what I'm here for. Have a great day!"

"You too."

Sara hangs up and contemplates what she has just heard. It is unclear whether various things make no sense because they do not make sense or because she has inadequate information. Consolidated Aerolithics is not a publicly traded company, so there would be no regular stockholder meetings or other regulatory scrutiny that would make the Perennas' absence conspicuous. Still, they would have had to make some decisions and sign something in the past six months, especially if the company was being sold.

If they were dead, she sees no reason why that would be kept secret. There is no upside to it. The story would be that Consolidated Aerolithics had become rudderless following the passing of the company's beloved founders. United Monolith is stepping in to shore the company up and continue the legacy, ensuring the dream does not die with them. If there were some issues with the circumstances of the couple's death, United Monolith could put the emphasis on learning from the tragedy and then touch on the improved safety practices and security measures they would be implementing. It is not rocket science but, even if it was, they have rocket scientists on the payroll.

The shield is even more nonsensical. She has the impression it was a throwaway suggestion Rehg made when he met with the mayor and it immediately became a thing. There was no study or thought put into the idea. It was just the mayor saying they have a museum by the Monolith with nothing worth showing in it and Rehg responding that the company has something worth looking at in storage he could have delivered. Maybe they chuckled over the hinge exhibit and decided the delivery had to happen before the new installation was in place. Promises made and shook on.

Tarik got the brunt of it. She can understand why he was

brusque when he found himself in the middle of the so-called illegal artichoke orgy. Still, she would have preferred dealing with that than the politics of the longer-term agreements. Not only does she have no time for it but there are no obvious partners she can work with. The hinges are going up anyway and she has no idea whether that is something she should be fighting against. Should she be laying the groundwork for United Monolith to take over and, further down the line, buy the building? Are other items in storage fair game for display? Is the shield a permanent gift?

While Rehg's intention of giving more back to the local community as United Monolith buys the crown jewel of local industry is obvious, nothing else fits. His apparent ignorance of and—when she reminded him—disinterest in the science-based initiatives already in place adds to the absurdity of it. The Monolith is effectively a science hub and the shield has absolutely no connection to what they do. She could, as he sort of suggested, make the museum science-themed. Given the size of the space, the first thing she would have to do is get rid of the shield, which would directly contradict the handshake deal with the mayor.

The announcement timing could change everything. Maybe there is no longer any point in thinking about the museum. Since the deal was so informal, there is no mechanism to change direction other than new instructions directly from Rehg. If she was Gail, she would wager Rehg had completely forgotten about it.

A knock on the door interrupts her train of thought. Gail walks in without waiting for a response. She sits down and immediately starts talking.

"The rumours flying around this place today are insane. I didn't start a single one all week, had it in my calendar to correct that oversight today, being Friday, but now I don't know. Seems like a waste; it'll get lost in all the noise."

"Rumours such as?"

"You've never been one to ask about such trifles."

"That's when they all came from you and I had a steady stream of anxious scientists coming to my office asking me to confirm or deny them."

"They must have given up. You weren't in your office all morning."

Sara sighs. "What can I deny for you today, Gail?"

"They're selling the Monolith. Plan is to turn it into condos."

"Smart move, to consolidate operations on the compound at the edge of town."

"So it's true? The commute's going to be murder."

"I have no idea." Sara had not thought about the real estate implications of buying Consolidated Aerolithics. Both companies have compounds and, at least for United Monolith, an increasing amount of business has already been moved out there. The change would make the museum even less important for them. She looks at her watch; fifteen minutes until the announcement.

"The big boss is supposed to make an announcement this afternoon. The scuttlebutt is we're getting into wind farming."

"Smart move. We'd be able to improve the integration of our battery stacks with electricity generation. How many times has storage been an afterthought? How many times has a client given us a call only after they discover it isn't windy all the time and people use air conditioning on calm days?"

"So it's true?"

Sara is tempted to say yes but is not that cruel. She knows Gail will go around making bets and end up losing beer money for her team. "I have no idea."

"Great help you are. Have you at least looked over the physicist posting?"

"Not quite finished."

"You seem distracted. Something must be up."

"You'll know when I do, in less than fifteen minutes."

"Hrmph." Gail stands and starts to leave.

"Thank you for all your work yesterday. Everyone really stepped up to pull off the presentation."

"Yeah, well, I may have bet we would fail but that doesn't mean I really want us to actually fail, if you get what I mean."

"I do and appreciate it."

Gail leaves and Sara clicks the link to the corporate site live-streaming Rehg's press conference half a world away. She refocuses on the posting, goes over it once more to make sure it follows the most recent corporate culture directive, signs it off and starts reviewing the next one in the pile. Her phone rings before she has a chance to finish the general description at the top. The display reads "Security." This bodes well, she thinks as she picks up the phone.

"It's Tarik Williams, we met earlier."

"What can I do for you, Tarik?"

"We have reason to believe there will be an incident at the museum tonight."

"An incident?"

"An incident."

"Meaning?"

"If you care to come down to the security control centre, I would be happy to give you a rundown of the situation."

Sara does not care to do anything museum-related. She cares to manage the Monolith Research Program; to work with some of the brightest minds on the planet to develop cutting edge technology and be at the forefront of what defines this Neolithic Age. Being tripped up by a sorry excuse for a museum and a mass of gold not being useful conducting electricity is not in the program. She takes a deep breath.

"I will be right there."

"It's in the basement, can't miss it."

She takes a last look at the screen before leaving her office. The camera is pointing at an empty podium beside what looks like a half-melted lump of platinum. When the elevator door opens at the basement level, she steps into a part of the building even more depressing than the dark side. The pale fluorescent lights have achieved complete dominance here, yet fail to wash out the greyness of the short walls cutting the open floor into countless cubicles, let alone liven the dark blue uniforms everyone is wearing. This level was set up for larger-scale experimentation until such functions were moved to the edge of town. She has not been down here since security took it over.

Walking toward the large, opaque box in one corner, she glances at the visible computer screens. Almost all show video of a variety of places, both interior and exterior. The blue-uniformed workers, some with headphones, are staring at the screens and typing notes. She cannot tell whether the scenes are live, recorded or a mix of the two. The box's door is open, so she does not hesitate to enter. Tarik and two others are sitting at a conference table in the middle of the room. Stations and screens are located around the periphery but are unmanned at the moment. One screen is showing the live-stream, muted. Rehg is now behind the podium, speaking to the crowd.

"Please close the door," Tarik says.

Sara complies and then sits at the table.

"I don't think Driss Rehg told you the whole story about the shield."

"Probably not."

"A year ago, a collective going by the name of Saint Glinglin managed to partially dissolve a statue in front of United Monolith world headquarters. We had known about them for quite some time but that was the most high-profile action they successfully pulled off. It was also a major embarrassment for the company and me personally."

"So, the shield is a trap."

"How did you...yes, it is. Though it is more than that. A museum dedicated to the neighbourhood the company razed is also a sore point. The shield is the first step in changing the story that's told."

"Why not just let it close?"

"From what I understand, if that happens the exhibits will be moved to the central museum and archives where they will be seen by even more people. This is doubly problematic since we have just purchased Consolidated Aerolithics."

"It's low risk. The items are not themselves important, historically speaking, according to the museum director. They might not even bother transferring them. If they did, the boxes would end up in storage somewhere, not on display. Still, that's not why we're here."

"No. We have been tracking Saint Glinglin since the platinum-statue incident. A cell has been active at a low level in this neighbourhood since it was redeveloped. They mainly paint murals. There has always been some chatter about blowing up the Monolith but nothing serious."

"You wanted to force their hand and provide a distraction for the acquisition." She gestures at the screen. "That's why the melted statue is in the frame. It might even provide for some sympathy for the company."

"Dissolved, not melted. Do not lose sight of the fact that Saint Glinglin has repeatedly attacked the company. They are also on several terrorist organization lists."

"That's why the security guard is out front rather than inside the museum. And that there's only one."

"Correct for the first point. Less chance they get hurt out front with people driving by. On the second point, a team is on-site."

"And cameras?"

"We are monitoring existing cameras. Unfortunately, we do not have any in the room. Saint Glinglin is moving faster than we expected. They will not be installed in time."

"Tonight?"

"Tonight. The local group has never done anything like this. We anticipated they would need time to plan. Instead, it looks like they are relying on out-of-town talent. Talent that has already arrived."

"But you don't know if it's actually happening tonight?"

"No. It's highly probable but not certain."

"And they are going to try to dissolve the shield?"

"Yes."

"The video my daughter took, the one you showed me this morning?"

"Your daughter is loosely affiliated with the local group but we have no reason to think she will be part of this. She seems to be a fan of, what is it?" Tarik looks to the uniformed woman sitting beside him.

"Boulderless bouldering," she says.

"Yes, that. Glinglin has put up bouldering walls in the neighbourhood. Your daughter frequents them."

"She has also been seen in the museum," the woman adds.

"Right, but only with the Perenna girl."

"Anna," Sara supplies.

"Who has no connection whatsoever to the group," Tarik explains. "We are not sure about Tony Abbott."

"We have no evidence he is linked," the woman says.

"But we do not know he isn't either. He seems to be, at the very least, highly susceptible to influence and morally ambiguous. Still, we are talking about Nadia. We did arrange for her video to be more popular and reach more members of the group. That is all. For obvious reasons, it is not in our interest to implicate her any further in the affair."

Sara thinks about asking for assurances, though she does not imagine for a second they would be worth much. Tarik is right that it is not in United Monolith's interest for the kid of a senior manager to be caught damaging company property. That, along with her fairly strong conviction Nadia is not stupid enough to get involved in such a hare-brained scheme, will have to do.

"What's my role here?" she asks.

"You are the senior manager at the Monolith," Tarik replies. "If anything happens tonight, there will be decisions to make. Even if nothing happens, you should be informed."

"Right. So the plan is to wait and react?"

"Yes. If everything goes well, the group will be caught red-handed."
"If things go badly?"
"A shootout in the main street."
"No chance the Monolith is the real target?"
"There is always a chance. We are prepared for it. There is also heightened security at the compound."
"Okay. Any other details? Can I go back to my office?"
"No and yes. I will call you as needed."
"Fine."

On her way back to her office, Sara wonders how dissolving a statue could be considered terrorism. It seems more like the act of a wacky cult, more dangerous to themselves because of their improper use of hazardous chemicals than to anyone else. What are the chances Nadia would join a cult? she ponders. By the time the elevator reaches her floor, she concludes she does not know her daughter well enough to say. It is an oddly comforting thought, as it means she is not deluded enough to end up being one of those parents on TV who always believed their child was an angel and incapable of committing whatever horrible act they just committed.

Sitting back down at her desk, she pushes thoughts of her daughter, the museum and the live-stream aside and starts reviewing the next posting from the beginning. She manages to get through the entire stack without major interruptions. While the phone rings several times, it is always someone needing direction or a detail on a research project. She moves on to a stack of budget adjustment requests as the light fades outside and her office begins to resemble the basement.

She leaves the office later than she would have liked but is still quite content. Tarik has not called, so the museum drama continues to be theoretical. The possibility of it makes her appreciate the organized tasks of corporate paperwork that fill so much of her time. Consequently, the nostalgia of working directly on research projects fades.

She texts Yi-Fu that she is on her way. He replies moments later, saying she might not be the last one home for once. A jolt of panic passes through her at the thought of not knowing where Nadia is tonight of all nights. It passes when her husband adds their daughter has been passing the day helping Anna come to terms with the news of her parents. Knowing Nadia would never respond in a timely way to a text from her, Sara asks Yi-Fu to confirm. After what Tarik said about Anna having nothing to do with Saint Glinglin, she is almost but not quite at ease.

The feeling evaporates when Yi-Fu informs her Nadia's phone is at the apartment. Their daughter is glued to her phone; something must be wrong. Sara starts her car when another text comes in. This time "Security" pops up, telling her something is happening at the museum and recommending she come back to the control centre. She sits there, thinking through her options, hands gripping the wheel. Then she turns off the car and goes back into the building.

The box is buzzing; the stations are manned, the screens show feeds from cameras up and down the main street. A large map is spread out on the central table and three more people have joined the group. The chair Sara sat in earlier is free, so, out of burgeoning habit, she sits there again and pulls out her phone.

"Reception is blocked in the box," one of the blue uniforms says. "You have to leave to make a call."

"Thanks." She leaves, sends a quick, somewhat obscure message to Yi-Fu, instructing him to not call anyone, and then returns. The conversation swirls around her. From what she can gather, they have someone stationed across the street from the museum. He has just been accosted by a passerby and the group is trying to decide whether it was a random person or Saint Glinglin there to distract him. This morphs into a critique of having an agent playing at being a panhandler at a location a real panhandler would likely never be.

The conversation is cut short when one of the operators at the edge of the room alerts everyone of three grey sedans caught on multiple cameras approaching the museum. Two of them look like Tony Abbott's car but they cannot be sure. Ten minutes later, an agent watching the back of the museum reports the arrival of a car. The box's main screen hooks into an infrared dash camera with a view of the action. Four figures exit the vehicle, two start working on the fence while the other two disappear. The voice informs the room they are making a lot of noise.

The guard in the front yard calls in to ask if he should go around back and check out the clamour. Tarik tells him to do it. Once he has left his post, operators report seeing the other two grey cars pulling onto the main street. The agent across the street advises them the cars have stopped in front of the museum and are being unloaded. Tarik orders one of the operators to tell the intervention units to be prepared to move in.

Then they wait. Sara looks questioningly at the blue uniform who let her know she could not use her phone in the room.

"We want them to set up their equipment before we go in," he explains. "That way, we'll have more evidence of their intentions later. Juries have a hard time understanding motivations that don't easily fit into the usual categories of greed, envy, wrath and the like. The sins they grew up with."

"Not that we don't paint them as envious," another uniform points out.

"True," the first agrees, "but that's marketing. It doesn't always go our way in the courtroom. A lot of people secretly want to see United Monolith taken down a notch or two. Tends to lead to hung juries."

"Greed works better."

"Right, but failing that terrorist and religious nut narratives are quite successful. Only, we need to show the jury pictures of the apparatus all ready to go to really sell a plan to liquefy several tonnes of gold."

The agent across the street mentions a figure approaching the driver's side of one of the cars, getting in and driving away. The lookout at the back informs the group a moment later of the car entering the museum parking lot. She also reports one of the perpetrators, all of whom scattered when the guard came around, had returned and is waiting in the first car. The group concludes Saint Glinglin will be escaping out the back. Tarik gives instructions for units to block off the ends of the alleys when the time comes.

A city police liaison officer enters the room, apologizing for being late. Tarik tells her she is just in time and brings her up to speed. Once everyone is on the same page, half the room empties out to join units on the ground. Sara finds herself in a black SUV with the officer, Tarik and a random blue uniform she has yet to hear speak. A series of SUVs leaves the Monolith and drives directly to the museum.

Continuous updates are channeled to Tarik in the car. Right before they arrive, he gives the order for the assault. The police officer echoes the direction to her people and the air is immediately filled with the light and sound of sirens.

"Something's not right," Tarik explains to the others in the car. "The terrorists are already running out the back. Something or someone must have tipped them off."

"How long were they supposed to be in there?" the police officer asks.

"Ask our scientist," Tarik responds, nodding toward Sara.

Sara is unprepared for the question, so takes some time to react. "I'm not an expert. Dissolving that much gold I should think would take a lot of time. They would need at least the weekend to make a noticeable impact. But we'd be talking weeks maybe, perhaps a lot longer... I don't know. Assuming they don't cut up the shield first to increase surface area and depending on the acid."

"Aqua regia," Tarik says, "seems to be their style."

"But they could leave and let the chemical do its thing," the officer suggests.

"That depends," Sara says. "I'm pretty sure the gold would still be there as a precipitate once the acid has decomposed. Unless they want to leave all the gold behind, they'd at least have to come back. I understand they don't want it for themselves but they have to know how easy it is to pour the residue into a mold to create another shield.

"But it's potentially even more complicated. The acid wouldn't keep dissolving the statue forever. With that much gold, it would lose its effectiveness and have to be replaced. I don't know how quickly; somebody would probably have to stay to monitor it. Doesn't sound like that is what's happening if they're running out. It sounds more like an accident. The HAZMAT team has been called, right?"

"Yes," Tarik responds. "We're here."

Sara exits the car with everyone else and sticks by Tarik's side. The senior police officer and United Monolith agent at the scene approach and inform the new arrivals of the developments. One of the cars was stopped at the end of the alley at the south end of the block and five people were arrested. A car managed to get past them at the north end. It has already been found in a parking garage at the edge of downtown. The suspects had scattered and a manhunt is underway. The third car, the same make and model as the one owned by Tony Abbott, was left behind.

The whole scene seems surreal to Sara. Lights are flashing all around her but the only sirens she can hear are far off. Officers and agents involved in the intervention have moved to control the perimeter, and probably join the manhunt, leaving the centre mostly empty. Media and miscellaneous onlookers are concentrated just outside the circle. Some of the cameras are pointed at the inaction, others at one of United Monolith's media relations people. The hazardous materials unit has yet to arrive, so the investigators are milling around their vehicle. She missed all the action and is not sure what she is officially responsible for. No one here works for her, so she feels like an obstacle people have to go around to reach whomever they do take orders from.

Tarik heads to the southern alley blockade with the liaison officer, so Sara follows. The United Monolith agent goes over how all the members of the cult who headed their way were arrested without incident and were already on their way to the police station. He hesitates and then mentions a girl who came over to ask them what was going on. She was a bit grubby and sweaty and was wearing dark, unassuming clothing.

"She said she was meeting a friend," he continues, "but if I were a young woman out on a Friday night with friends, those aren't the clothes I'd be wearing. All the cultists had on that sort of unremarkable clothing—nothing specific but it was sort of noticeable with them all grouped together. She came up to us from behind and was talking to Pete, so at first I thought nothing of it. After I had some time to reflect, I ordered her to come back and she ran off."

"We went after her," Pete continues the story, "but a block and a half later it was like she disappeared. We weren't supposed to leave our post, so we called it in and came back."

"What did the lieutenant say?" the liaison officer asks.

"He asked if we were sure. We said 'no' and that was that."

"We thought you should know," the agent says. "Might still be able to find her if we leave now. I don't think anyone else is coming down the alley."

"Probably homeless," Sara says. "Curious but scared of authority. She went south?"

"Yes, ma'am," Pete replies.

Tarik looks at Sara for a second with narrowed eyes. Then he turns to the liaison officer. "If it's okay with you, we can pull my agent and he can join the manhunt downtown."

The officer nods.

"But sir..." the agent protests.

"We need bodies downtown, where we are sure some of the suspects are. That is the priority. And, as the head of the Monolith says, the girl is most likely homeless. Given our complete failure to have an agent play a panhandler tonight, I am not inclined to trust the opinion of my team on the subject of the downtrodden. If I were a betting man, I would wager it was that failure that tipped off the suspects. So what will it be: stay here or go downtown?"

"Downtown, sir."

The group has already started to walk up the alley by the time the agent responds. Sara is sure she raised Tarik's suspicions by saying what she did. She still pulls out her phone and sends a text composed of a compass and a thumbs down symbol to Yi-Fu. When she looks up, she notices Tarik studying her. He looks away without a word and engages the liaison officer in conversation. They pause behind the museum, then head back to the main street around the northern end of the block.

The HAZMAT truck arrived in their absence, along with various people in business attire. Sara recognizes members of the mayor's office, the local councillor and the head of the main street business association. Every ounce of her wants to don a protective suit and join the HAZMAT team in neutralizing and disposing of the chemicals. Instead, she pauses and turns to Tarik.

"Can you get an update on the situation and then join us?"

"Of course."

She appreciates how quickly Tarik picks up the lay of the land, despite his likely unfamiliarity with local personalities outside of Saint Glinglin. Tarik and the liaison officer go over to the crime scene and HAZMAT technicians. Sara joins the notables as the personification of United Monolith, a corporate pillar of the community whose invaluable gift to the city has just been targeted by criminals.

13

Helen answers the door when Tony rings the doorbell.

"Simon's in the kitchen," she says, leading him to the living area on the second floor. "I hope you like leftovers. There's a ton from yesterday."

"I'm happy nothing's going to waste. What do you want to do with this?" He raises the bottle of wine in his hand.

She thanks him and takes the bottle. Once they reach the room, she grabs a corkscrew lying around, opens it and leaves it on the coffee table to breathe. Simon yells something unintelligible from the kitchen.

"He probably wants me to carry something," Helen says. "Do you want anything to drink to start?"

"I'm not picky."

"I'll grab you a beer," she disappears, coming back a couple minutes later with a platter, a beer and a laden Simon in tow.

"Thanks for inviting me," Tony says as an initial toast, clinking glasses.

"It was actually Anna's idea," Simon informs him. "Occasionally, she takes time out of her fish-jesus obsession to think of others."

Both Helen and Tony protest the characterization.

"To Anna!" Simon says to cut them short. They echo him and glasses clink once more.

"You should turn on the TV," Tony suggests.

"What, really?" Simon asks.

"Today might be even crazier than yesterday."

Helen finds the remote and presses the "on" button. The screen shows Driss Rehg, standing behind a podium and beside a sad-looking statue, answering questions from the press.

"That's a great question, one that's posed to most technology companies. The pat answer others give is they don't know where or how the metals are mined because of the intricacies of their supply chain. By the time the cobalt and other materials reach their manufacturing facilities, they are already several steps away from the mine.

"With the acquisition of Consolidated Aerolithics, United Monolith has direct interest in the mines. This not only means a guaranteed, uninterrupted source of material for our products with minimal price fluctuation, it means we will be able to ensure the safety and security of miners. If there is any child labour being used in these mines, it stops now."

"Your parents' company uses child labour?" Tony asks Simon.

"I don't have any idea. I hope not. I didn't think my opinion of them could get much worse but that would do it."

"If they didn't, that was a masterstroke," Helen says. "United Monolith looks great and they don't have to spend money eliminating something that doesn't exist. All they need to do is have some NGO inspect the mines in three months and take very public credit for improvements they never had to make."

"Wait, hold on, what's going on?!" Simon exclaims as he absorbs exactly what Rehg said.

"You heard it right," Tony replies. "United Monolith just announced they bought Consolidated Aerolithics."

"Does that mean my parents have surfaced?"

"I haven't heard anything about them."

The three watch the screen intensely, as if willing the camera to pull back and show more of the scene. They imagine a row of chairs on the stage off to one side where the rest of the participants in the deal are sitting. The camera obstinately stays tight on Driss Rehg and the partially dissolved sculpture.

Rehg continues to answer questions but the focus is exclusively on United Monolith products. Details about the new generations of permanent magnet motors and batteries arouse the most interest. Besides the existing mines, nobody seems to know or care about what Consolidated Aerolithics does. The primary purpose of the company, to develop technology for mining celestial objects, is completely lost. Helen ends up muting the sound.

"As I said," Tony says to break the silence, "today could end up being more fantastic than yesterday."

"Consolidated's a private company, isn't it?" Helen asks.

"Yup," Simon replies.

"Does that mean you and Anna would inherit it if your parents passed?"

"No idea. For a couple fixated on the future, they weren't particularly concerned with ensuring their legacy. At least when it had anything to do with their kids. I wouldn't be shocked if they left their part to someone they know well and I have never met in my life. Hell, it could have been Driss Rehg. Uni-lith has the resources and the motivation to keep the space-mining program going. I can't imagine what I'd do with it."

"Sell it to United Monolith? Be set up for life?"

"That makes sense. If I ever become CEO of some unwieldy corporation, my first move will be to bring you on as an advisor. Then I'll fire all those no-good child labourers, with their wee little fingers and creepy dead eyes."

"You need to raid their pension fund first," Tony suggests. "No way that thing's sustainable."

"Some saint you are!" Helen cries.

"Our actuarial tables show low life expectancy," Simon states, "at least for the ones who do twenty-four hour shifts. The solution is obviously to step things up for the lazy eighteen hour shifters. And raid the fund anyway. Maybe take the company public, set up a shell corporation to do a leveraged buyout and suck the business dry. Cherished advisor, what do you think?"

"Somewhere in there," Helen says flatly, "you have to promise someone the moon."

"So, we can conclude my parents clearly erred in not leaving me the family farm."

"Clearly," the other two echo.

"Food!" Simon reaches for a large chunk of chicken breast on one of the platters in front of them.

"Should we wait for your sister?" Tony asks.

"Yeah, it seems wrong to start without Anna," Helen adds.

"Shit, I should have texted her when Tony arrived," Simon says. He pulls out his phone.

Helen and Tony's attention is drawn to the television screen, where Driss Rehg and his sculpture have been replaced by the flashing lights of emergency vehicles. They look closer.

"Isn't that the main street?" Helen asks.

"I think so," Tony replies. "Turn up the sound."

The announcer talks breathlessly about an emerging situation on the street. First reports are of some sort of break-in at a business behind him. Suspects have apparently been apprehended.

"What are the chances someone stole the shield?" Helen wonders.

"This soon? I don't think so. That thing isn't exactly portable."

Simon puts his phone down: "It's got to be the shield."

"There are a lot of stores and other businesses on the street," Tony says. "It's more likely a hold-up for quick cash. You couldn't even fence the shield. It would have to be melted down, sold as ingots or something. The effort, the equipment required..." He shakes his head.

The announcer declares new information is coming in. The break-in supposedly occurred at the local museum. He turns and addresses someone off camera, evidently having no idea there was a museum there and uncomfortable saying whatever he is supposed to say. Still unsure, he looks back at the camera and informs viewers it concerns the city's Museum of Artifice. Once they get the gist, Helen lowers the volume but does not mute it.

"I stand corrected," Tony says. "The shield is the only thing there anyone could possibly want. But it still doesn't make any sense."

"You were the one saying today is going to outdo yesterday in the strangeness department," Helen points out.

"That I did."

"Well..." Simon starts.

"Not more Saint Anthony stuff," Helen interrupts. "This is real!"

"...it was a massive temptation, like the embodiment of temptation; pure, refined temptation."

"But so impractical," Tony says.

"When you get to that level of temptation, practicality isn't really a thing."

"Apparently not."

"Maybe the museum's going to close after all," Helen speculates. "Shouldn't you go to the scene, Tony?"

"It sounds like they caught the perps," Simon counters. "The shield probably hasn't even been moved. Uni-lith security did its thing. Why would the museum be closed?"

"Helen's right," Tony says. "They'll re-evaluate the risks of having something so valuable at the site and conclude it's better to keep it at the central municipal museum. Or Uni-lith will just take it back, display it at the Monolith or something. It was a pretty stupid idea to put it there in the first place. And," he takes a long sip of beer, "best not show up with alcohol on my breath. If someone needs me, they'll call."

"I bet Uni-lith had their reasons; there's some logic to it we're missing."

"The logic is to make people forget about the old neighbourhood. The City has wanted to close the museum for years and politicians were finally getting on board. If there was any reticence left, it's gone now."

"Doesn't this sort of thing put a spotlight on the museum and, by association, the old neighbourhood?" Helen asks. "It seems counterproductive."

"People will be blinded by the gold," Simon argues.

"Uni-lith's generosity will be front and centre," Tony agrees.

"So, the museum's going to close after all," Helen repeats.

"Guess so," Simon says. Tony nods without a word.

They hear the door open and close.

"Anna's here!" Helen says.

"Finally! I'm starving," Simon proclaims. "Anna, hurry up! The food's getting cold!"

"It's already cold," Tony points out the obvious.

"Shoosh."

Simon's words have no impact on his sister, who takes a detour to the bathroom before coming up. When she appears, she is holding Buddy Merchrist in one hand. As it cannot stand, she shifts some platters and lays it on the coffee table.

"Okay," Tony says, "the bizarre quotient went up another notch."

Simon forgets about the food and picks up the figure. "You finally found a fish-jesus. I have to say it is some quality work."

"In the spirit of making it a unique symbol," Anna says, "I have christened it Buddy Merchrist."

"Makes sense." Simon passes it to Helen. "So, now what? You're going to become some genius artist? An iconoclast of some sort?"

"Someone was whining about starving to death."

"I was not whining."

"He was getting petulant," Helen interjects, putting the figure back on the table. Tony nods in agreement.

"Fine, we'll eat."

Anna belatedly notices the television, which is looping "What We Know Now" museum interludes between segments of serious-looking talking heads prognosticating about the future of United Monolith and short clips from Rehg's press conference.

"Foiled burglary at the museum, is what they're saying," Helen says.

"Not a burglary," Anna responds.

"Oh?"

"Saint Glinglin."

"Of course!" Simon says, slapping his forehead. "Why didn't we think of it?"

"That does explain things," Tony adds. "They're not concerned with taking and fencing the gold. But still..."

"But still?" Simon asks.

"Why? Sure, it's Uni-lith property, a symbol of the company, but it's not like the sculpture from the press conference. It's not really prominent. Why take the risk?"

"And also," Helen continues to bring Anna up to speed, "United Monolith has acquired Consolidated Aerolithics."

"Have you heard back from the embassy?" Anna asks Simon.

"Not yet."

Anna finally sits down. The three reflect on how tired she looks.

"You weren't involved, were you?" Simon grabs the piece of chicken he had been coveting.

Anna shakes her head. Helen and Tony take Simon's cue and start in on the platters.

"You'll feel better once you've had something to eat," Helen gently nudges Anna.

"Consolidated is dead?" Anna inquires of no one in particular.

"From what I gather, it's going to be a division of Uni-lith."

"A new and improved Consolidated!" Simon announces between bites. "Now with fifty percent less child labour!"

"Don't pay any attention to your brother. Your parents' dreams aren't dead."

Anna does not comment. She takes a small carrot from the edge of a platter and nibbles at it without enthusiasm. The three others look at each other and silently agree to change the subject.

"Simon tells me I owe tonight's invitation to you," Tony says. "Thank you!"

Anna looks at the carrot, thinking about what she is doing and pops the whole thing in her mouth. "We were the ones who lost the communal pig; it's the least we can do."

"It would have been wrong to leave you all alone with so much temptation," Helen says, playing along.

"You just know if greed has made its way into your sanctum, the other sins can't be far behind," Simon adds. "Remember, no matter how much you eat, leftovers are exempt from gluttony."

"If you say so," Tony smiles. "Yes, better to be among the heretics than the sins. Sins are so one-dimensional. Buddy Merchrist is far more interesting than a golden shield."

"Right?" Anna says with more energy. "Adam got him for me. Dunno where but I don't care. It's inspired."

"Inspiring you to become an iconoclast?" Simon asks.

"You're only saying that because you like the word," Helen points out.

"Oh yes, you're absolutely right. There's no question about it. Doesn't mean it's not a great idea."

"Encouraging your sister to become a heretic, and not just an academic, theoretical sort of heretic? I mean, it's all good fun to play at Tony being Saint Anthony but I'm starting to believe the school counselor. You're not the greatest influence. Saint Glinglin is an iconoclast. Imagine if she joined up with them. She could be in jail right now and headed off to prison for who knows how long. Is that what you want?"

"We're talking about music or art or whatever it is she's working on. Not breaking into a building to dissolve a megalith. Context is important and she's smart enough to know where the line is."

"I'm sitting right here," Anna says.

"You know where the line is, right? I'm not that irresponsible, am I?"

"Saint Glinglin doesn't work."

"Okay, but more generally?"

The doorbell rings.

"You should get it," Helen tells Simon.

Simon nods and heads downstairs. He opens the door and finds himself face to face with Yi-Fu. He knows Yi-Fu is Nadia's father—they have met several times—but he is never sure about his name, despite receiving a text from him the day before. Not really knowing the name of his sister's best friend's father is not a great indication of responsibility.

"Is Nadia here, by any chance?" Yi-Fu asks.

Simon shakes his head.

"Anna?"

Simon calls back, "Anna, can you please come to the door?"

An awkward silence settles in until Anna arrives.

"Hi Yi-Fu," she says, sensing something is wrong but unsure how much she should say. Technically, she does not really know if her friend was part of the group at the museum tonight.

"Hi Anna. Any idea where Nadia might be tonight?"

"No. She isn't answering her phone?"

Yi-Fu pulls his daughter's phone out of his pocket.

"Oh. Have you tried Martin?"

"Do you know where he lives?"

"Not exactly."

Yi-Fu frowns. "Any reason she might be around the museum?"

"No. It's closed. Tony, who runs the place, is here. Thankfully, really, from what I see on TV."

"He's here?"

"He already had a couple drinks when we got wind of the burglary, or whatever it is," Simon explains, "if you're wondering why he isn't at the scene."

"Thanks," Yi-Fu says distractedly, his mind already elsewhere now this possibility is checked off the list.

Once the siblings have returned upstairs, Simon lets the others know Nadia appears to be missing.

Seemingly out of the blue, Anna blurts out, "Buddy Merchrist is a symbol of why Saint Glinglin doesn't work."

"It wasn't already clear by the fact they have a manifesto that boils down to boiling down corporate statues?" Simon asks rhetorically.

"I almost had it when Adam gave Merchrist to me," Anna continues, ignoring her brother's sarcasm. "But now it's so obvious. At lunchtime, when I was looking up the background, it was all about the son killing and replacing the father. It was an endless cycle."

"Freudian, probably."

"Sure, anyway, so what good does it do to dissolve all those statues, to take down the corporations? That will just create a vacuum that needs to be filled. What if the next corporations or dictators or whatever are much worse?"

"The French Revolution leading to Napoleon," Tony comments. "It's a common critique of revolutions."

"How does Merchrist fit in?" Helen asks.

"In the Saint Glinglin myth, there's a machine that makes it sunny all the time. The son breaks the machine, making it rain and dissolving the statue of the father. Things happen; water, wetness, flooding. In the end the son sacrifices himself to make the machine work again. He is so obviously the Merchrist."

"Okay..." Helen gives Simon a look saying plainly this flight of fancy is all his fault.

"Well, good," Simon says. "We shouldn't go around starting revolutions and killing our parents. Of course, the whole killing our parents thing is probably an academic, theoretic sort of exercise for us. Regardless, lesson learned."

"However," Tony tempers, "we don't want to be fatalists either."

"True, it's more of an ends-don't-justify-all-means lesson. Society should be made better, only there are limits to what we can justify doing to bring it about. Within those limits, we should try even if at the end of the day we might not succeed. Is that about right, my cherished advisor?"

"The problem with all this talk about lofty ideals is that it often hides real suffering," Helen adds.

"Exactly," Anna says. "I'm completely on board."

"Really? It sounds kind of like you'd be okay with Saint Glinglin if it wasn't for the endless cycle."

"Maybe I would be but that doesn't matter because it does repeat."

"What if destroying the machine meant blowing up the Monolith? or assassinating Driss Rehg?"

"It depends. I wouldn't rule out any of that if I knew it would really accomplish something. But it won't."

"It's the Georg Elser conundrum," Tony suggests. "He almost succeeded in taking out Hitler and a number of other high-ranking Nazi party members before the war. His bomb did kill people, just not the right ones. Was he justified in making the attempt?"

"Let's make a rule to not encourage assassinating anyone," Helen says.

Tony is about to reply when his phone rings. "The call arrives, not from the City or the police, but from the United Monolith Corporation. Why am I not surprised." He goes into the kitchen to respond.

"Tarik Williams calling. We met yesterday."

"Yes we did."

"You have probably heard about the incident at the museum."

"Just what's on the news."

"Can you join us at the scene?"

"It's Friday night. I'm not exactly sober."

"Okay. Nonetheless, I would like to run through a couple things tonight. We can do it over the phone. Tomorrow, we can walk the site."

"Any reason I'm not getting this call from the police?"

"If you want to talk to them, I can arrange that. This is being treated as a joint investigation between United Monolith and municipal authorities. They will however insist the conversation happens at the station and you provide a written statement. I would hate to ruin the rest of your evening."

"What do you want to know?"

Tarik prefaces his questions with a rundown of the situation. Effectively, it was Saint Glinglin attempting to dissolve the shield, the shield suffered minimal damage and about half the suspects are in police custody. He emphasizes the word "police."

"You do not seem concerned about the theft or destruction of anything else at the museum. Why is that?"

"There's nothing of much monetary value at the museum except the shield. The symbolic value is also fairly low. I'd wager there was more damage done last night."

"You would lose, unless the skylight costs less than the artichoke flower."

"The skylight was broken?"

"One pane."

"Has anyone put up a tarp?"

"I will make sure it is done. See, Mr. Abbott, this conversation is useful for both of us. Is there any reason the Glinglins would want to implicate you in the crime?"

"Nothing comes to mind. Why?"

"Two things. First, they used grey Honda Accords."

"Probably because no one would look twice if they saw one in the parking lot."

"Your vehicle has not been stolen?"

Tony looks out the front. "Nope."

"Second, they didn't break in."

"What about the skylight?"

"That has not been completely ruled out but is unlikely. There is no sign of a rope, for instance."

"The straps?"

"Possible, along with jumping on the shield. However, the first team in heard the glass shatter on the floor. More likely someone escaped through the opening than entered through it. Who has a key to the building?"

"It's a municipal building, so lots of people. I imagine building operations or City security can give you a list."

"Have you given a key to anyone?"

Tony hesitates and starts pacing in the kitchen. "Only my assistant."

"Who is?"

"Anna Perenna. You didn't know that she was my assistant?"

"Why did she need a key?"

"She frequently did work before school started, before I arrived."

"Why is she your assistant?"

"Is she a suspect?" He paces faster.

"Not at the moment. Why is she your assistant?"

"Her school arranged it. Extracurricular activities are expected, or at least highly encouraged."

"At the museum?"

"It might surprise you but some people actually care about history and the preservation of the city's heritage."

"Are you aware of an incident at the school involving a broken window?"

"What does that have to do with anything? She has been nothing but helpful at the museum. That's what counts in my eyes and should be the only thing that counts for you."

"Forgive me for my directness but she has exhibited deviant tendencies and has recently learned her parents passed away."

Tony stops dead. "Whose fault is that? You're the one who burst into the museum last night and created a mess. You're the one who left a mass of gold there, for Christ's sake, and you're surprised bad things happen."

"Please calm down, Mr. Abbott. Would Anna have copied her key or given it to someone?"

"No. Good evening."

"Thank you for your help."

Tony bites back what he wants to say, takes a deep breath and another beer out of the fridge. He then rejoins the others.

"Are you a suspect?" Simon asks.

"He can't be a suspect," Helen points out. "He's been here all evening."

"A patsy, maybe," Anna suggests.

"Since we are apparently anti-murder tonight," Tony says, "I'll keep my thoughts to myself. Do you have your key to the museum, Anna?"

Anna gets her key ring, which she left on the console by the front door, and dangles it in front of him. "Why? Do you want it back?"

Tony shakes his head.

"They were asking about Anna?" Helen looks worried. "She hasn't been here all evening."

"It's routine," Tony reassures her. "She does volunteer at the museum, so of course they're going to ask."

"I can't decide which one of you would make the better fall guy," Simon states, "the off-kilter adolescent with a weakness for cults and a history of violence against property or the grizzled bureaucrat resentful of the forceful imposition of corporate interests representing a level of power and wealth denied to him his whole life."

"We could be in cahoots," Tony says, the tension from the phone call draining from him.

"Oh, I like that word too."

"So, I've decided we have to steal the gold," Anna forcefully brings the conversation back to her.

"Why do you think that?" Helen asks.

"As I was saying, Saint Glinglin doesn't work. But the Glinglin everyone talks about is the fringe. Nobody mentions the murals, the boulderless bouldering Nadia likes or any of that. It's just like everyone is talking about the shield and seems to have forgotten the entire neighbourhood is the way it is because Uni-lith forced their way in and made it their own."

"The story is a touch more nuanced," Tony interjects.

"But, as Helen pointed out, it shouldn't only be about the music, the competition. It's like we're playing their game; for or against the company, they're always the centre of attention. The Monolith never lets us forget they're king of the hill. So, we start a band and make it about creating stuff together."

Simon looks amused, Tony bemused and Helen concerned. Each almost says something at different points but holds back.

"I don't mean really starting a band of course. Also, the whole creativity thing is out. All I can imagine are space goats..."

"Space goats sound fun," Helen says, trying to sound encouraging.

"My creativity, I mean. It's shit. But we can support others. We can get rid of some of the ugliness in the neighbourhood. We can resist some of the negativity of Uni-lith without crossing the line."

"Stealing could be considered crossing the line, Anna."

"Yeah, go back to the stealing part," Simon adds.

"The golden shield is like the original model of ugliness. It's garish and completely useless."

"It is shiny though."

"As if it was pure gold," Tony adds.

"It represents one of the worst parts of Uni-lith and it doesn't belong in the museum," Anna continues.

"That last part, I agree with."

"Let's make something beautiful with it. Not us, but let's put it out there for others to use."

"I'm intrigued," Simon admits. "How?"

"Turn it into paint. Not all of it all at once; a bit at a time."

"Where did you get this idea from?" Helen asks.

"Does it matter? What if I came up with it?"

"It's not a good path to start down."

"Won't Uni-lith security notice?" Simon asks, before answering his own question. "Unless we took it from the inside."

"Simon, you aren't helping."

"There are the piano straps," Anna says.

"Won't work," Tony points out. "A grand piano is, what, a tonne and a half at the outside? The shield is at least ten times that. We'd have to reinforce the roof. Come to think of it, I'm surprised it hasn't fallen into the basement."

"Not you too." Helen shakes her head.

"Really?" Simon asks. "This might be an ignorant question but how did the forklift get it in there? Can a forklift carry that much weight?"

"You didn't notice the rails last night?" Tony replies. "The forklift wasn't lifting, just pulling the crate along the rails."

"Huh. I did not notice them at all. That sucks. I was imagining hollowing it out to the point where all that was left was a wafer-thin skin, maybe held in shape by a frame like you use for Artie. Then, months or even years later, Driss Rehg comes to visit and inadvertently pokes a hole. He is shocked, makes the hole bigger to figure out what's going on and the whole thing collapses. I'm picturing the reaction of the warden in Shawshank Redemption. That would be poetic."

"That would be great."

"Can you guys come back to earth for a moment?" Helen asks.

"Okay," Anna says, "No piano straps. It doesn't matter; it was probably damaged tonight."

"It was," Tony confirms, "according to the head of Uni-lith security."

"So, they won't notice if some more gold is scraped off. The weight will already be off if some of it was dissolved."

"Gold's soft," Simon addresses Tony. "You could bump into it with a cart or something to throw them off."

"And then what?" Helen asks, trying a different tack. "You sell it to artists?"

"We give it to the mural Glinglins," Anna replies. "They do what they've always done, only even better. Nadia took me to a mural mausoleum this morning that was so incredible. It was like the only place I could start to really process the news of mom and dad. It was all blue and white and gold, and so intricate. Only, the gold wasn't so great. It was almost orange. Imagine what they could do with real gold paint."

"If that's the plan," Simon points out, "I'm not sure we'd even be stealing. Uni-lith owns the checkerboard buildings, so technically they would still have the gold."

"We'd be damaging their property," Tony says.

"It's what they get for leaving a valuable object in a sorry excuse for a museum, I'm sorry to say. Anyway, we'd also, indirectly, be improving some of their property."

"But they're going to close the museum," Helen states.

"No way," Anna retorts. "Uni-lith can't afford to back down after tonight. That would be begging for Saint Glinglin to step up their attacks."

Silence descends on the group. Up until this point Tony and Simon viewed the idea as a thought experiment. Helen knew if they worked it through they would pass beyond theory and tried without success to nudge them from this path. All of them realize at the same time Anna's plan could really happen. Anna profits from the lull by taking handfuls of food from the platters, having evidently found her appetite.

"Are we actually thinking about this?" Simon asks quietly, suddenly timid in speaking his mind.

A moment passes before Tony responds. "I will try to get you a very small amount of gold. You," he looks at the three others in turn, "figure out how to turn it into paint. If we can manage that, we figure out a way to get it to the mural Glinglins without it coming back on us."

All eyes turn to Helen. "I can't believe you'd talk about all this in front of me! I don't want any part of it! Anna, think about how this could ruin the rest of your life!"

"The rest of my ticky tacky life?" Anna asks, mouth full.

"At least we aren't talking about murder or blowing up the Monolith," Simon argues. "It's actually fairly reasonable as far as these sorts of things go."

"I'm sorry, I can't stay any longer," Helen declares and walks to the top of the stairs. She looks back with a melancholy expression on her face, seems to be about to say something more but thinks better of it and descends.

"So..." Simon intones after they hear the front door open and close.

"I guess I'm not much of a saint after all," Tony says.

"Dunno," Anna remarks. "Trading greed for beauty seems pretty saintly to me. Making the checkerboard a nicer place to live isn't nothing and you're not exactly harming anyone."

"And we did lose the communal pig," Simon adds.

14

Yi-Fu stares at Sara's text, "Don't call anyone." Nadia is in trouble is the message and for some reason calling the police is out of the question. He turns off the heat under the stew he is preparing and starts heating up the stovetop coffee pot. Going to the computer, he glances at the news. Stories of the acquisition of Consolidated Aerolithics dominate the feed. Nothing reported gives him a hint as to where his daughter might be. Taking a half-full daypack sitting by the entrance, he adds a variety of potentially useful items. The pot whistles; he pours the coffee into a thermos and takes some granola bars from the cupboard. Once they are added to the bag, he puts on walking shoes, a medium-weight jacket and hesitates at the door. Turning back, he grabs Nadia's phone, leaves a quick note and strides out of the apartment.

The checkerboard is quiet. An occasional siren rings out, the low hum of traffic from major roads nearby is constant. On such a cool evening, people are mainly indoors. A patchwork of apartment windows are lit up, either giving a glimpse of the interior or highlighting a wide variety of coverings. Even with the streetlights, toys and other objects left out on front lawns have become amorphous and dull. A corner of the Monolith is visible from the street, a solid block that anchors everything around it.

Yi-Fu's approach is methodical. While he knows about Martin, the boulderless bouldering and all sorts of other aspects of his daughter's life, he does not have a great sense of the where of any of it. He pauses at the end of the walk, then starts walking up and down each street and between each building on the board, a flashlight to illuminate dark corners in hand. He passes small groups of what he generally calls kids heading to the bars on the main street or, more ambitiously, the clubs downtown, and dog walkers.

At every encounter, the temptation to show them a picture of Nadia and ask if they have seen her is almost overwhelming. But if Sara warned him against calling the police or anyone else, how is asking people in the street any different? He is already taking a risk by looking for her himself but he cannot do nothing. Sara would know that though. His rational mind's recurring reminders his daughter could be tied up or who-knows-what in any of the many buildings he passes are forcefully pushed to the back.

When he reaches the pile of boxes that is the school, he remembers the story of Anna accidentally breaking the window. Given Nadia's habit of climbing things, he decides it is worth checking the roof. He drags a garbage can to the edge of one of the smaller boxes, flips it and tries to climb up. Failing to pull or swing himself up with his bag, he reluctantly leaves it leaning against a wall. He struggles to get up even without it and, once he finally manages, is forced to pause before rising to his feet. He spends the moment on his back contemplating how old he feels and gazing at the orange glow of the sky.

Nadia is the one who likes heights, climbing them and descending at dizzying speeds. She rarely complains about their cross-country ski outings but he knows she would prefer downhill, ice climbing and everything in between. He finally gets up, avoiding looking over the edge, and explores the roof. A small can partially filled with butts and random debris is the only sign people continue to gather since Anna's incident. As he approaches the edge of the box where the can sits, the occasional siren multiplies and becomes an enduring cacophony.

His first thought is that a neighbour saw him on the roof and called it in, but it quickly becomes evident the sirens are not approaching the school or anywhere in the checkerboard. He finds his way to the other side of the roof, on a different box, and sees a concentration of flashing lights on the main street. Checking the news on his phone, stories of a suspected burglary have taken over the top spot from the acquisition. He searches for any mention of hostages or casualties but the reports are all vague two-liners with "more to come" or equivalent at the bottom. He is somewhat relieved at the lack of details. It gives a sense he still has time.

Leaving the school grounds, the regimented walk continues. He passes through two boulderless bouldering locations, a cave, pyramids, ziggurats and other murals he does not linger long enough to figure out. The checkerboard always seemed to him plain, geometrical and utilitarian. The street trees, as evenly spaced as they are, have been the only part of the neighbourhood to give him any pleasure. It is only now, after years spending his days at the United Monolith compound at the edge of the city and his weekends far out of town, he realizes how little he knows about the neighbourhood.

Nadia talked about it from time to time but he never took it all that seriously. Up until tonight, she was a typical teenager who rarely raised her eyes from her phone. Given the constant tension between her and her mom, it made sense to him to turn everything into a joke and lighten the mood. That she still went skiing and hiking with him, without having to be dragged out of the house or blackmailed, was a sign their relationship was working. Every mural he sees is painful, as if it is not only a hidden part of the neighbourhood he never took the time to seek out but also an unknown facet of his daughter. Maybe he still has time but he worries the opportunity to get to know her better has already slipped away.

Regardless of his increasingly dispirited thoughts, he continues on. He recognizes the Perenna home as he passes by. At first, it seems like another interaction Sara would want him to avoid. Nadia was not in school today because she was supporting Anna however, so he makes an exception and hopes for the best. Perhaps he can make an exception for all her friends, if Anna can tell him where they live. Perhaps Nadia has been here the whole time. He feels less and less sure of anything. All he knows is the lights are on and someone is inside. Walking to the door, he checks the news feed to stabilize himself and discovers the burglary occurred at the museum.

Simon answers after he rings the bell. Yi-Fu tries for nonchalance, as if he just happened by and was curious where his daughter was. She had left her phone at home and he knew how important it was to her. Suddenly having to talk to people throws him off. He still manages to find out Nadia is not there and Anna is as ignorant as he is as to where she might be and where Martin or anyone else lives. Even before the end of the short conversation, as soon as it becomes clear his search must continue, his mind skipped ahead to contemplating how to efficiently search the foothills next-door.

Only after walking away is he hit by his callousness. He is so fixated on finding Nadia it did not even cross his mind to say something supportive concerning Anna's and Simon's parents. Anna seemed less brittle than she had been during her confrontation with Sara but it was obvious she was not her old self. Not that being her old self a day after hearing the news would be a good sign either. He promises himself to call or visit on the weekend, so long as the situation with his daughter does not take a turn for the worse.

The train of thought does not slow his progress. Before long, he finishes combing the checkerboard and comes around to the main street a couple blocks north of the museum. Leaning against a wall, he checks the news once more. He skips over most of the new details, singling out that a number of suspects are now in custody and there is still no mention of hostages or casualties. As he scrolls, a passerby stops in front of him.

"What an unfortunate mess," the passerby says, nodding in the direction of the museum.

"Yeah. It's especially low to steal from a museum."

"Eh. Yesterday, it was a Museum of Artichoke; today a Museum of Artifice. This'll just give the 'A' hole who runs the place an excuse to come up with another nonsensical 'A' word."

Yi-Fu looks up, not believing his ears. "I guess..."

"But look at all those big booted bastards tramping across the front yard. Inconsiderate imbeciles—at this rate we'll never get any blue flowers come spring."

"You could plant some..."

The passerby is already walking off, shaking his head.

Yi-Fu moves on to the foothills. He starts strong but has more and more difficulty keeping his doubts at bay. Instead of possibly being in each building he passes, Nadia could be in another neighbourhood entirely. She could have been abducted and is right now tied to a chair in a barn somewhere in the countryside. Sara could be negotiating with the kidnappers while he pointlessly shines his flashlight into random dark corners. His whole enterprise seems absurd as he is completely in the dark.

The search continues in spite of his mounting uncertainty. The motivation for his movements shifts from hope to inertia. Even the inertia starts to vacillate with the uneven blocks of the neighbourhood. In the checkerboard, there was no hesitation as to his path. Here, he has to choose which way to go, leaving an opening for even more questions. He checks the time and sees several hours have gone by. Nadia could have come home in the meantime; she could be worried about him. It takes him a panicked second to remember he left a note in case she or Sara came back.

His phone rings, making him jump and drop the flashlight. He reacts quickly, catching it in midair. Then he looks at his phone, finding another obscure text from Sara. A compass and a thumbs down. Without hesitation, he heads south, no longer checking every corner for signs of life. What exactly he should be looking for is unclear but he trusts his wife. It will become obvious in due time.

The route south ends at the promenade, so he slowly walks along it. A conversation drifts over about a "fella wearing dark clothes" jumping the railing. He freezes, knowing instinctively the figure had to be Nadia. He turns to the people talking, a couple old men sitting on one of the benches.

"I'm sorry to interrupt but I couldn't help overhearing something about someone going over the railing. That's insane! Did it happen tonight?"

"Yeah," one of the men replies.

"Just over there," the other adds, pointing to the railing about five benches down.

"I bet it was a circus," Yi-Fu says, "with police and ambulances and everything."

"Nah," the first says. "Just one police car."

"And a helicopter," the other adds.

"Right, and a helicopter."

"They didn't find anything though."

"There's trees down there."

"They just shone their lights down there for a bit, gave up and left."

"Didn't even go down and search."

"Guess they had other things to do."

"Maybe they'll come back tomorrow, when it's light out."

"The fella who fell over'd probably be dead by then."

"I wager he's already dead. And he jumped, clear as day."

"Wow," Yi-Fu interjects. "I bet you don't see that every day." He walks to the railing and shines his flashlight on the slope.

"Don't see that every day 'cause it's a terrible spot to kill yourself," the second points out. "More likely he broke some stuff and rolled down the hill a ways. I bet he'll bleed out by morning."

"We could've told you you wouldn't see anything."

"I did already, what with the police doing it and giving up."

"I wasn't looking for a body," Yi-Fu says, "just signs someone rolled down there. To see if you're right."

"Have to wait 'til tomorrow to know for sure," the second remarks.

"Yup," the first agrees.

"Fair enough," Yi-Fu admits, starting to walk away. "Have a good evening!"

He keeps his measured step as hope increases. The talk of

death does not faze him—even though he cannot be sure whether Nadia could have made the jump and managed the slope without injury, he is convinced she did. His daughter is not Anna, after all. He heads to the west end of the promenade in search of an easy way down, passing in front of countless benches. They are increasingly empty as people retire for the night or take refuge from the falling temperature.

The well-worn goat path he finally finds takes an oblique angle down the slope into the woods. It might be a path he has taken before, picking up litter as part of spring clean-up, but everything looks very different at night. Before starting down it, he fishes a headlamp out of his bag and dons it. There is no way he is doing this without both hands free. His steady rhythm is replaced by carefully placed steps. The orange-tinged night of the city is slowly left behind, replaced by the sharp contrast between the cold white LEDs of his lamp and the blackness of everything beyond their reach at his level and below. Looking up, the city's glow is ever-present yet immeasurably far away.

The sky is obscured when he reaches the trees. The second step in, his foot slips on the mud and he falls backward. Grasping a trunk, he is able to right himself before he is too far gone. He curses and tries to continue with more caution but that proves impossible. The only way to be more cautious would be to stand still or follow the lead of the police and come back tomorrow. Instead, he uses the muddy momentum for a series of controlled slides.

The path, such as it is, goes deeper into the trees, making it difficult to situate himself in relation to the neighbourhoods on the other side of the railing. Not that he completely trusted the accuracy of the people who told him where the "fella" went over the railing but it still seemed better than nothing. The problem is compounded by the difficulty of shining a light into all the crannies up- and down-slope while keeping his balance. As in the neighbourhoods, he accepts the limitations of his search. The inadequacies still weigh on him.

The monochrome world is soon disrupted by the wavering orange light of a campfire. He approaches, if only to escape from the darkness for a time. Four young people wrapped in assorted clothing and blankets, easily the age of those he passed heading to the bars and clubs, are sitting around the flames, apparently mesmerized. Yi-Fu's gait returns to something resembling normalcy as the ground flattens and becomes drier. All eyes slowly turn to him and they shift to give him room to join the circle. "Welcome," a large man with an unkempt beard says dreamily. Yi-Fu expects suspicion and receives unquestioning hospitality. He wonders if the anxiety of the evening undoubtedly written all over his face makes it obvious he could use some warmth.

Warmth has to wait however. He stays standing and sizes up his audience. Then he gets straight to the point.

"Did any of you hear someone come over the railing tonight?"

"Yeah," the first answers.

"We all did," the second adds and all four nod.

"Did you go check it out?" Yi-Fu asks.

"No," the third responds.

"We don't want any trouble," the second says and they all nod. "It didn't take long for a helicopter to show up. A helicopter's always bad news."

"Bad news," the fourth echoes.

"We thought the police would be down here, scouring the woods," the first says.

"Some cops'll use any excuse to hassle us," the second explains.

"Evict us," the third adds.

"Confiscate our stuff," the fourth says.

"We don't want any trouble," the second says and they all nod.

"Can any of you point out the direction?" Yi-Fu asks.

They all point to the east, on the other side of the camp from where Yi-Fu arrived, with various levels of conviction. The first jerks her thumb over her shoulder, the second twists his body and extends his arm out, the third waves the beer can in his hand and the fourth points the index finger of one of her hands resting in a supine position on her lap. Yi-Fu figures everyone has the same desire to help but each is working with a different level of energy and drive.

He thanks them and passes around the camp. As he is about to leave the aura of light and warmth, the second speaks up.

"Do you need help?"

The offer takes Yi-Fu by surprise. Talking and pointing is one thing, actually going out into the darkness is another altogether. He is about to decline but pauses to reflect on the chance any of them would talk to or be questioned by the police. They evidently consider law enforcement hostile and so something to avoid. He weighs the risk, looks once more into the darkness and decides to accept.

"What's your name?" Yi-Fu asks.

"Led. You?"

"Yi-Fu. It's pretty muddy. Are you sure you'll be fine?"

"I've seen worse."

"Flashlight?"

Led shows him an old flashlight and points a weak beam at a tree. Yi-Fu considers giving him new batteries; he knows he has a bag of them somewhere in his pack. Instead, he hands Led his own flashlight and starts to feel selfish, keeping the headlamp for himself.

"Does the person we're looking for have a name?" Led asks.

Yi-Fu hesitates again before responding, "Nadia. But please don't yell it out."

"Got it. Let's go!"

Led, free from the fire's hypnotizing effects, crashes recklessly into the woods, slips, gets up yelling "I'm okay!" and then moves forward with a little bit more care. Yi-Fu takes a parallel route. It is indescribable how much better he feels to no longer be alone in his search. He senses Sara has been with him in a manner of speaking the whole time. Only, she has not been beside him to experience every step, each more difficult than the last, leading him to this point of accumulated disappointment and fragile hope. Without her, he would not be so close to finding their daughter. She is where she needs to be. Right now though, it is Led and the constantly advancing light just off to the side that gives him the strength to stay in the game.

They pass by two more camps; one with a tent, the other a mass of sleeping bags and blankets under a tarp tied to the trees above; and various piles of garbage and impromptu toilets. In a moment of distraction, Yi-Fu wonders if there will be more to clean up this spring than in years past. Led does not signal anything unusual about the camps. The light to the side disappears again as Led slips for a third time, calling out a second later, "I'm good!" This time, when the light reappears, it does not immediately start moving forward again.

"I think I found something!" Led calls out.

Yi-Fu's heart skips a beat. "Don't do anything!" he calls back, forcing himself to not try to run to where Led has stopped. He knows nothing about Led and would be a fool to believe this stranger he just met has stumbled onto Nadia. Yet at each camp passed, he has counted on Led's judgment. Every patch of ground Led has checked as they moved through the woods has been an area Yi-Fu has not searched himself. In trying to rein in his hope, Yi-Fu tips too far the other way and lands hard in despair.

Yi-Fu joins Led and drops to his knees beside a vague outline of dark fabric and hardened mud. He assumes the head is upslope and has to shift down when he realizes he is wrong. Wiping hair and mud away from the face, he recognizes Nadia. Finding her breathing and pulse are regular, the pendulum swings the other way.

"'Led'," he says as he pulls a blanket out of his pack and wraps it around his daughter. "Is that the metal or the past tense of 'lead'?"

"Past tense of 'lead.' Sometimes, when people make fun of me, they say I'm dense or heavy like lead. The joke's on them though. When World War Three comes along over all those fancy metals they need for everything these days and the nukes start flying, I'll be right as rain."

Yi-Fu checks for injuries and then fishes a scarf out of his bag. He wraps it around his daughter's head, avoiding as best he can putting pressure on the obvious bumps and leaving the ends loose on either side. Shifting once more, he immobilizes her head with his knees weighing down the ends.

"We were doomed the minute people started calling this the Neolithic Age," Led continues. "Do you know what that means? It means the Stone Age. It's when people started to get the hang of making tools. There was no metal or anything back then. It's when all those famous cave paintings were done. Here we are, with all our fancy doodads, and someone convinces the world this is the real Stone Age, and that stone is golden. Foreshadowing, man. That's what it is. We're all going to be back hunting and gathering, those of us who survive the nukes."

Yi-Fu opens a first-aid kit and takes out a capsule of smelling salts. He double-checks that Nadia's head cannot jerk up and breaks the capsule under her nose. An instant later, her eyes flash open and she gasps, as if she is coming up from underwater.

"I hear ya, Led," Yi-Fu says. "So, there I was making dinner yesterday and my daughter—this is my daughter, by the way—starts talking about ghosts in the old hospital. It was like this weird idea about being absorbed into a place if a person lived there long or deeply enough. I don't know, it was weird, and I remember it because her friend Anna's usually the weird one. My daughter is more into foolishness, like jumping over railings into ravines and that sort of thing.

"Anyway, she says to me she wants to just live her life and then be done with it. Makes sense—who'd want to stick around and haunt the checkerboard of all places? So, no absorbing of essences. Yesterday, all was clear; today, all is mud. It takes all of one day for her to practically imbed herself into this forest. A couple more days and she'd start to sprout, at this rate.

"I know what you're going to say, Led: teenagers, hormones, whiplash as a way of life. And, again, I hear ya, Led. I do. But yesterday I felt like we connected. We were of like-minds about the pompous silliness of megaliths. Of course I knew it wouldn't last but, you know, Led, would an extra day or two of feeling like I actually know who my daughter is be too much to ask?"

Nadia groans and tries to reach down to hold her head. Her right arm makes the journey, her left proves uncooperative. She seems unaware she is spreading mud where her father had wiped it away a moment ago.

"These woods're full up with ghosts already," Led responds, "no matter what the cops and the good citizens do to clean it out. Sleeping rough ages you. Every night here's like, I dunno, a month in your own bed, in your own home. Your life's seepin' into the soil. Doesn't seem to do the trees much harm; can't imagine it does 'em much good though. It's the sort of life that'd survive the nukes; the sort that has nothing extra to give."

"That's pretty depressing there, Led," Yi-Fu points out. "I know I'm grateful for your help. You're a good person. When the nuclear apocalypse comes, you'll still be going out of your way to give others a hand. That's the life essence you'll always have with you."

"About knowing your daughter, I dunno, seems like the changes in mood are who she is too."

Nadia slowly gets a handle on her surroundings. "Dad? Dad, is that you?"

Yi-Fu shifts around, takes off his headlamp, shines it in his face and smiles at her. "Nads, seems like you've had a bit of a spill." Addressing Led, "She hates when I call her 'Nads' but really, she's practically a plant right now; what's she going to do?"

Led says nothing, uncomfortable participating in Yi-Fu's off-colour jokes under the circumstances.

"I'm so embarrassed," Nadia says weakly.

"As you should be. Everyone knows helmets are mandatory equipment for railing jumping. Your head's become the definition of hard knocks."

"Please stop."

"So, what hurts? Anything numb? I need diagnostics."

"I'm perfectly fine. Just need to rest for a while." She moves all her limbs with mixed success and starts to slide further down the slope. Yi-Fu and Led stop her progress.

"No issues with your neck? Can you lift your head?"

Nadia raises her head and winces. "My head kills but everything else is okay."

"If we help you, can you sit up?"

She nods. "Don't touch my left arm."

Yi-Fu and Led carefully lean her against a tree and cover her again with the blanket.

"Lift the arm."

She is able to raise it to chest-height, then drops it. Yi-Fu unrolls the scarf and repurposes it as a sling. Led holds the first-aid kit open so Yi-Fu has easy access to the alcohol, wipes, bandages and all the rest. Once all the visible wounds are cleaned and wrapped, he checks there is nothing hidden. Nadia starts to nod off.

"Nads!" he calls out. "No sleeping now, not yet!"

He goes back to his pack and pulls out the coffee and granola bars. He offers a bar to Led first, who accepts. Then he makes sure Nadia drinks and eats. All three end up leaning against trees, munching and passing around the coffee. When everything seems calm, Yi-Fu texts Sara a thumbs up and a tree. Receiving "SR?" in return, he sends another thumbs up.

"I'm so sorry," Nadia says, the caffeine making her more alert.

"For bringing some excitement into my boring adult life? For giving me the opportunity to meet Led? There's nothing to be sorry for. Although if you rail jump without a helmet again, I'll disown you. To be clear."

"It's not great to be down here at night," Led says to Nadia, "especially someone like you."

"Yes, please heed Led's wisdom."

"I know, I will," Nadia says.

"This wasn't to get out of skiing tomorrow, was it?"

"What? No. We already weren't going skiing, because of Anna's parents."

"You can tell me if you don't want to do that anymore."

"I know."

"We have to keep talking."

Silence follows. Yi-Fu hands out more granola bars.

"I'll miss these after the apocalypse," he says wistfully.

"You probably wouldn't survive," Nadia points out.

"Led'll miss these after the apocalypse."

"It's true," Led agrees.

The three sit a while longer, giving Nadia time to regain her strength.

"Can you walk?" Yi-Fu asks after the food has been eaten.

Nadia gets up slowly, holding on to the tree. She closes her eyes tightly and grips the trunk tighter, making an effort to stay upright before sliding back down.

"I can't; everything just goes out of focus, wavers."

"Painful?"

"I can get through the pain; can't keep my balance."

"Can I ask you one more big favour, Led? We only need to get to the service road at the bottom of the slope."

"I'm not sure I'll be much help. I've fallen I don't know how many times on the way here."

"Have to chance it. As peaceful as it is, we can't stay here all night." Yi-Fu packs everything in the bag, carefully rises and puts it on his back.

"Yeah, okay."

They stand on either side of Nadia, Led on the right and Yi-Fu on the left. She grits her teeth and forces herself back up. She places her right arm over Led's shoulders, Yi-Fu grips her waist. They slip from tree to tree, following the single beam of the headlamp, the two men taking the brunt of the succession of impacts.

"I'm starting to rethink the wisdom of helping people," Yi-Fu says after smacking into a tree with the weight of three people. "It's really a painful experience."

Led waits for Nadia to respond, since the comments seem like part of their repartee. She is too busy however concentrating on not becoming a dead weight or throwing up.

"It'll be easier when most people are dead," he says.

"They'll certainly complain less."

The three reach a clearing with a gravel road running through it. Yi-Fu lowers Nadia to the ground and Led takes his lead. Yi-Fu goes to the road and looks in both directions, effectively signaling with his headlamp. A car starts and approaches from the west. The headlights are blinding in the relative darkness.

The car stops in line with Yi-Fu and Sara jumps out. The two make their way back to where Led and Nadia are waiting. Sara wordlessly drops down to Nadia's level and hugs her gingerly, tears streaming down her face.

"Thank you again," Yi-Fu says to Led, shaking his hand. He gives him the headlamp and the first aid supplies from his bag. "For the Stone Age."

"It's not like I want the real Stone Age to come again," Led responds, taking them. "We just seem to be asking for it. I hope your daughter ends up being alright."

"She's strong. Her shoulder didn't even pop out of its socket. Seriously though, thanks. I never would have found her without you."

"Oh, you would've. You, both of you, would've kept going 'til you found her. Still, happy to help. You're good getting her in the car?"

"We'll manage. Good night, Led."

"Night, Yi-Fu." Led dons the headlamp, stuffs the supplies into a pocket and goes back into the trees. Yi-Fu follows the light with his eyes, content to see steady movement until it is swallowed by the forest.

He turns toward his family and hears Sara whispering to Nadia that it is going to be alright. He touches his wife's shoulder. She looks up, her eyes sparkling, and nods. They help Nadia into the back seat of the idling car, cover her once more with a blanket and drive home.

ABOUT THE AUTHOR

Trent Portigal is a writer of eclectic curiosities based in Edmonton, Canada. Previous books include Simulated Hysteria *(2020),* Death Train of Provincetown *(2019),* The Amoeba-Ox Continuum *(2017) and* A Floating Phrase *(2016).*